Dina glanced at her watch. Her roommates had probably already gotten back to the hotel and were soaking in the hot tub.

"I'd planned to stay, at least until you went to Radiology, but I guess I could stay longer, if you want me to."

"Don't want to take your time."

She sent him a gentle smile. "Don't worry about it. I'm a nurse, remember? I'm used to hospitals and working the late-night shift."

He fixed his gaze on her and almost looked as if he wanted to tell her something but wasn't sure if he should.

"What? What is it?" she asked, curious but not wanting to pry.

He hesitated, then answered in a whisper so soft she couldn't be sure she'd heard him right. "You're scared? Is that what you said?"

He nodded.

"There's nothing wrong with being scared," she told him, wanting so much to console him. "You wouldn't be human if you weren't. But usually things don't turn out half as bad as we imagine they will. You have to believe you'll be fine."

What else could she say? What could she do to comfort him? Even though he was a bull rider and had no one to blame for his injuries other than himself, what she wanted to do was wrap him in her arms and tell him he would soon be back to his old self. But that would be a lie. Until the results of the X-rays were read and the severity of his injuries known, there was no way of knowing much of anything. He might recover fairly quickly, or he might end up like. . . She shuddered at the thought. *No, not like my father!* Just thinking about that possibility made her stomach quiver. Grasping his hand in hers and holding it tight, she decided to do what she should have done in the ambulance. Pray.

JOYCE LIVINGSTON loves to write and feels writing inspirational romance is her God-given ministry. A wife, mother, grandmother, and former television broadcaster, she has many life experiences from which to draw. Her books have won numerous awards, including Heartsong's Contemporary Author of the Year in 2003 and 2004, and Book of the Year numerous times. She has well over twenty books in print, and more contracted and in the writing stage.

Books by Joyce Livingston

HEARTSONG PRESENTS
HP353—Ice Castle
HP382—The Bride Wore Boots
HP437—Northern Exposure
HP482—Hand Quilted with Love
HP516—Lucy's Quilt
HP521—Be My Valentine
HP546—Love Is Kind
HP566—The Baby Quilt
HP578—The Birthday Wish
HP602—Dandelion Bride
HP618—One Last Christmas
HP626—Down From the Cross
HP637—Mother's Day
HP649—The Fourth of July
HP658—Love Worth Keeping
HP665—Bah Humbug, Mrs. Scrooge
HP698—With a Mother's Heart
HP705—Listening to Her Heart
HP713—Secondhand Heart

The Groom Wore Spurs

Joyce Livingston

Heartsong Presents

A note from the Author:
I love to hear from my readers! You may correspond with me by writing:

Joyce Livingston
Author Relations
PO Box 721
Uhrichsville, OH 44683

ISBN 978-1-59789-930-7

THE GROOM WORE SPURS

All scripture quotations are taken from the King James Version of the Bible.

Our mission is to publish and distribute inspirational products offering exceptional value and biblical encouragement to the masses.

PRINTED IN THE U.S.A.

one

Unpleasant thoughts plagued Dina Spark as the endless, barren miles of Nebraska's West I-80 ticked by on her car's odometer. Every ranch, every herd of cattle, every fence post brought back memories of the way her rancher father had been before a wheelchair had become his prison and his only lifeline to mobility. He had known the risks and been more than willing to take them, regardless of the costs to him and those around him. "What price we humans pay for glory," she proclaimed aloud with a shake of her head.

She glanced at a road sign as it whizzed past her window, then at her watch, before leaning back in the seat to enjoy the remainder of her ride. This extended weekend at her friend's house was exactly what she needed and she was going to enjoy every minute. Thirty miles later, when she came to the familiar little town of Chitwood, she signaled her turn and headed south, eventually making a left onto the road she thought was the one to take her to Burgandi's house. After driving nearly another fifteen miles, and the country road morphing into nothing more than two dusty tire tracks, she realized she was hopelessly lost. In near panic, she scanned the road ahead of her, looking for a safe place to turn around when, suddenly, the engine died and her car came to an abrupt stop. *Oh, no. This can't be happening! I have no idea where I am!*

Instinctively she did what she always did when faced with a problem, closed her eyes and prayed. But, even then, the car refused to start. Frustrated, she pulled her cell phone from her purse and dialed Burgandi's number, hoping she and her father would come and help her. But that idea, too, proved futile, as the message on her phone's screen read NO SIGNAL.

The heat from the afternoon sun bore down on her, turning her perspiration into outright beads of sweat. They trickled down her forehead as she exited her car, lifted the hood, and peered at the many belts and gadgets that normally kept her car running smoothly. Other than checking the battery terminals, she had no idea what else to do. Maybe she could walk to a farmhouse and they could call Burgandi for her. But after sheltering her eyes from the blinding brilliance of the sun, she realized there wasn't a farmhouse in sight. Hot, annoyed, and very much alone, she climbed back inside to contemplate her options. Walk or stay in the car until someone happened down the road, which might be hours.

Walking won.

Yanking her keys from the ignition, she placed them in her purse and was about to sling its strap over her shoulder and roll up the window when she heard the faintest sound of an engine. Glancing over her shoulder she saw a truck of some sort wending its way toward her, leaving a curly trail of dust in its wake. As it came closer, she could plainly see its worn paint job and cracked windshield, as well as numerous dings and dents. The old truck looked like a junkyard reject. Why hadn't she brought the can of pepper spray her mother had suggested?

She sat, half grateful, half in fear, as the truck came to a stop a few feet behind her rear bumper and the driver emerged, his face nearly hidden by a voluminous scruffy beard, and wearing worn clothing that didn't look much better than the truck. She was about to reach for the lock button and raise the window when the man walked toward her.

"Got car trouble?" he asked simply.

She nodded. "Yes. It quit on me. It won't start."

He tugged at his stained ball cap, pulling it lower on his forehead. "Don't you know this road doesn't go anywhere? It dead-ends down there a mile or so, where the old bridge finally washed out. Didn't you see the sign?"

What sign? Had she missed it? "No, I guess I didn't. I was looking for the Leyva place."

He frowned, or so she thought. It was hard to tell with that full beard and his ball cap pulled low. "No Leyvas on this road. You must have made a wrong turn."

"Maybe. It did seem like I drove more miles after I turned off at Chitwood than the other times when I've been in this area."

"Don't feel bad. The roads around here can be pretty confusing." He gestured toward her hood. "Did you check your battery terminals?"

She nodded. "Yes."

"You didn't run out of gas?"

"No, my gauge is still showing a quarter of a tank."

He moved to the front. "Pop your hood. Let me take a look."

She pressed the hood release then climbed out and stood watching over his shoulder as his hands moved capably from one area to another. If he didn't know what he was doing, he had her fooled. After a few minutes he lowered the hood, letting the latch engage with a snap. "It kinda looked like the connection on one of your battery terminals was a bit loose, so I tightened it. Jump in and see if she'll start."

She crawled in and gave the key a turn. Nothing. If he hadn't been standing there she would have cried. "How far is it to the nearest repair shop?"

"One that could fix a car like yours? Maybe twenty miles."

Dina leaned against the headrest with a sigh of defeat. "Is there a farmhouse nearby where I could call someone? My cell phone isn't getting a signal."

"Yeah, I know. Mine isn't, either," he said slowly, as if contemplating the nearest place. "The Coulter ranch is about three miles from here. I could take you there."

While his offer was generous and she appreciated it, she was still afraid of him. What if he was telling her that her car was unfixable so he could lure her into his truck and take her to some even more isolated spot? No one would ever know he was the one who had picked her up. "But if you want me to take you, you'd better hurry. I gotta get back and do my chores."

Frazzled thoughts ran through her head. Normally, she would never crawl into a truck with a stranger, but it appeared she had no other choice. "Thank you," she struggled to say, still not sure what she was about to do was wise. "I'd appreciate a ride to the Coulter place."

She grabbed her purse from the seat and, as an afterthought, the small case containing her makeup and a few other things she hated to leave behind, locked her car, then followed him to his truck.

After opening the passenger door he went to work brushing the seat off with the palm of his hand. "Sorry about the mess," he told her as bits of straw, paper, broken Styrofoam cups, empty pop cans, and a few things she didn't recognize fell out onto the dirt road. "It's usually not this bad."

Without a word of response, she climbed inside, cradling her bag and her purse in her lap.

He rounded the truck and climbed into the driver's seat, slamming the door three times before it finally caught hold. She grabbed the armrest as his truck backed over the ruts and headed in the direction they'd come. They rode in awkward silence for quite some time, which was just fine with her.

Finally, he said, "I take it you're not from around here."

"No. I'm from Omaha."

His gaze left the road long enough to give her a half smile. "Omaha, huh? Big-city gal?"

"I guess you could say that. I used to live in Farrell, a small town northwest of there, but I moved to Omaha after. . ." She paused. He didn't need to know her family history. "When I went to college. I'm a nurse."

"Good profession. I guess a nurse could live about anywhere and find a good-paying job."

She nodded and then, despite the heat, quickly rolled up her window, the dust from the road nearly gagging her. "Yes, I guess I could."

"Me, I'm a rancher."

"You enjoy it?"

"Oh, yeah. It's a hard life, and some years the pay is lousy, but I couldn't live in the big city like you. I have to have the wide-open spaces. It's not much farther to the Coulter place."

That was good news. Despite the kindness he'd displayed so far, she was anxious to get out of that truck and call her friend.

"Too bad you couldn't have broken down closer to civilization. Hardly anyone uses that old road. I haven't been on it in months myself, but I wanted to check out a piece of property down by the creek I heard might be for sale."

"I'm glad you came along." And she was glad. Now that they were near the Coulter place, most of her fear had subsided and she'd begun to think of him more as an angel sent from God than the villain she'd been afraid of when he'd first come along.

The Coulter ranch turned out to be a lovely place. A woman came out onto the porch and waved as his old truck rolled to a stop in her driveway.

"Brought you a damsel in distress," he explained good-naturedly as he helped Dina exit the truck. "Her car broke down out on the old Bennington road. I did all I could to get it started but nothing worked. Our cell phones couldn't get a signal. We hoped she could use your phone."

"Of course she can." The woman motioned to Dina. "Come on inside where it's cool. You two look like you're about to melt."

He lifted his hand. "Thanks, Mrs. Coulter, but not me. I gotta scoot. Got chores to do."

Before Dina realized it, the man had climbed back in his truck and started the engine. With a wave, he was gone, and she hadn't properly thanked him or even asked his name.

"You're mighty lucky Will happened down that road," Mrs. Coulter said, smiling as she closed the door behind the two.

Dina nodded. "Yes, I am. I'm sure he was sent by God."

Mrs. Coulter spun around, her brows raised. "By God? Does that mean you believe in Him?"

Dina smiled proudly. "Yes, ma'am, I do."

The woman smiled back. "I'm mighty proud to hear that. That makes us kinfolk. The phone is right there on the table."

❧

Will checked his watch. He'd have to hustle to get everything done before he headed out for his long weekend. But he was glad he'd taken time to help that woman. He was just sorry he hadn't been able to get her car running. Too bad such a rotten thing had to happen to her. She seemed like such a nice person. Pretty, too. He wished they had exchanged names. Not that it made any difference. They'd probably never see each other again. But it would have been nice to think of her by name and not just as the nice woman he'd tried to help.

He pressed the accelerator closer to the floor. He had to put all thoughts aside and concentrate on his own weekend.

Because being distracted in his line of work could cause things to happen that never should. His mind needed to be clear, with his thoughts totally focused on what he was doing. Anything else could bring injury, or maybe even worse.

two

Burgandi grinned at Dina as the two friends floated on the creek on their air mattresses the next morning. "I'm glad you came. I've missed you."

"I'm glad, too. Getting to spend time with you was well worth the long drive. But I have to admit I was terrified of that man when he stepped out of that truck, looking like he did."

"Other than his scruffy appearance and your description of his dilapidated old truck, you haven't told me much about the man himself. How old was he?"

Dina giggled. "I have no idea. With that heavy beard, I couldn't see much of him. I can't believe I missed my turn."

"Some of the road signs out here are so faded they're hard to see."

Burgandi took a cautious step onto the rickety dock at the creek's edge then tossed Dina a towel. She caught it and wrapped it, turban-style, around her wet hair.

"That's what Will said."

"I thought you said he didn't tell you his name."

"He didn't. That's what Mrs. Coulter called him. I wish I would have asked his full name, his address, too, so I could have sent him a thank-you card."

"Do you realize it's only three weeks until our committee meeting in Cheyenne?"

Dina nodded. "I know and I'm excited about it. I've never been there before."

"Me, either." Burgandi picked up their bottles of suntan lotion and her own towel. "Come on. We'd better hurry. Mom's probably got lunch ready."

By the time they got back to the house, Dina's car was sitting in the driveway. Burgandi's mother smiled as she greeted them. "Guess what the mechanic found? Your gas gauge had stopped working. You only *thought* you had gas. Of course our little repair shop didn't have a one in stock. You'll have to have a new one installed when you get back to Omaha. But they filled your tank and set your trip meter at zero, so you'll know when it needs filled again."

"No wonder it quit on me! Where is Mr. Leyva? I want to thank him."

"He's out in the barn. He said to go on without him. By the way, Dina, how is your father doing?" Mrs. Leyva asked as the girls sat down at the table.

Dina fingered her napkin. "He's about the same, and I guess always will be."

"Is he bitter about his accident? So many people who suffer injuries that incapacitate them like that tend to get bitter."

"He's not only bitter, he's vindictive, arrogant, hateful and, worst of all, he takes out his anger on my mom. I hate him for it. If it wasn't for wanting to be with her, I'd never go to that house."

"Dina, don't talk that way. He *is* your father!"

"But, Mom," Burgandi pled on Dina's behalf, "he brought it on himself. Dina and her mother begged him to give up bull riding after that first brush he'd had with death and he wouldn't. If he didn't care about himself, he should have cared about his family. He's in a wheelchair for life. He can't even go into the bathroom without someone's help."

Dina hesitated, unsure she wanted to admit what she was about to say but forged ahead anyway. "I took it as long as I could before I moved out and got my own apartment. I tried to assume some of Mom's responsibilities, but he wouldn't let me. He said it was her *duty* because she'd vowed to take care of him for better or for worse when she married him. Get that? It was her duty, as if he owned her."

Mrs. Leyva's hand went to her chest. "I—I had no idea."

"As a Christian, I know I shouldn't harbor such bad feelings toward him. He wears his disability like an award for bravery but I see it as punishment for not listening to his family and quitting while he was ahead. That's why I've made myself a vow that I will never, ever, date a man who has anything to do with rodeos. I refuse to end up like my mother."

"But, Dina, you used to be a barrel racer."

She lowered her gaze. "Yes, I did. In fact I had hoped I'd get to be good enough to someday win the regional finals. But that all ended the day my father got hurt. Although injuries in barrel racing are pretty rare, it does happen. I decided then, the risk of being injured wasn't worth the thrill and the excitement of winning. I just wish my father had realized it before he ended up in that chair."

"But, dear, very few are injured as seriously as your father," Mrs. Leyva countered. "Rodeo is a sport. A lot of people here in western Nebraska take part in rodeos."

"That's true. Some rodeo events are fairly harmless and participants rarely injured, but those events don't attract as many dedicated fans and spectators as bull riding. Why? Because people like to see someone put their life on the line. If they took the bull-riding event out of rodeos, the attendance would drop considerably."

"Mom, if you'd seen how Dina's dad has changed since his last encounter with a bull, you'd understand why she feels the way she does. That man is nothing like he used to be."

Mrs. Leyva took Dina's hand. "From what you say, I assume he isn't a Christian. It sounds as if that man desperately needs the Lord. Considering the way he's confined to his home, you and your mom may be the only ones who will be able to reach him for Christ." Dina felt a slight squeeze on her hand. "Think about it, honey. Keep the door open, if only a crack. He may be all you've said, but he is your father."

As if eager to change the subject, Burgandi tugged on Dina's free hand. "Speaking of fathers, Mom has Dad's lunch in the oven. Why don't we take it out to him?"

Dina sent a gentle smile toward Mrs. Leyva. "Thanks for the great lunch, Mrs. Leyva. I especially loved the salad."

❧

It was nearly ten thirty the following Monday morning before Dina was able to take a break at the hospital where she served as a nurse in the trauma unit. Two shootings, a drug overdose victim, and a man whose arm had been badly mangled in an industrial accident had taken up most of her time since she'd reported to work a little before seven. She twisted the lid off the juice bottle she'd selected from the vending machine and took a long, cool, refreshing sip. It tasted good. On impulse, she stepped outside and pulled her cell phone from her purse, turned it on, and dialed Burgandi's number. "Hi, sweetie, I just wanted to thank you again for our wonderful weekend. I had a great time." She could almost see her friend's smiling face on the other end.

"Hi, yourself. I loved having you here. How's it feel to be back to work?"

"Good. This has really been a morning. How's it going for you?"

"Busy. I was about to call you. I just heard from Celeste about the committee meeting we'll be having in Cheyenne. She had a request for us."

"What kind of request?"

"She explained that each year during the planning session for our convention the chairperson arranges for those on her committee to perform a number of public service hours in whatever city we're meeting. She said the media is always eager to cover things like that, and it's a great way to let people know what's happening in the field of nursing. Since you and I are both on the planning committee, and both nurses in emergency-type areas, she asked if the two of us would mind volunteering."

"To do what exactly? I hadn't realized we'd be doing anything except working on next year's convention plans."

"She gave me a few examples from last year, when the committee met in Atlanta. Two nurses helped with the administering of flu shots to senior citizens; a couple spent several evenings helping a new industrial plant set up their first-aid facility. I think she said one or two others assisted by passing out brochures in a kiosk set up in one of the local shopping malls."

Dina shrugged. "If it means you and I will be working together, tell Celeste to count me in. Sounds like fun."

"Great! I was sure you'd say yes."

"Dina! Come quick!"

She turned at the sound of her name to find one of her coworkers hurrying toward her, and from the expression on his face she knew it was anything but good news.

"Bad accident out on 680! The ambulances will be arriving any minute."

"On my way, Jim!" Dina tossed her juice bottle into the trash can near the doorway then hurriedly said into her phone, "Sorry, sweetie. My break's over. Incoming emergency. Gotta go. See you in Wyoming."

❧

Awestruck was the only word Dina could think of to describe the way she felt as she sat in Cheyenne's Nagle Warren Mansion's parlor, waiting for Burgandi to arrive. The entire place was far more grandiose than she'd expected, from its ceiling-high mirror above the magnificent cherrywood fireplace to its lovely Aubusson rug. The brochure she'd found on the table said the mansion had been built in 1888 by Erasmus Nagle and later purchased by Jim Osterfoss, who had turned it into the present bed-and-breakfast establishment.

"Hi, girlfriend. Can you believe this place?"

Dina spun around to face her friend. "Hey, hi. I was beginning to wonder when you'd get here. When you told me Celeste had been lucky enough to get us into one of Cheyenne's nicest B and Bs, I never expected it to be this nice. I can hardly wait to see our rooms." Her eyes narrowed as she suddenly sobered. "But—nice rooms or not—if I'd had any idea the Cheyenne rodeo would be going on at the same time as our meeting—I might not have come."

Burgandi reached out and gave her a hug. "That's why I didn't mention it. But, buck up, kiddo. One more day, and this year's rodeo will be history. Besides, you and I aren't here to be entertained. We're going to be stuck in meetings for the next four days."

"Whew, I had no idea the Saturday morning traffic would be this bad. I didn't think I'd ever get here."

The two turned in unison as a pretty redhead with a soft-sided briefcase tucked under each arm hurried toward them.

"The others are already upstairs in our suite." Celeste nodded toward the elegant cherrywood stairwell. "I haven't had a chance to tell you why we're staying in such a luxurious place. Mr. Bellows, a wealthy man who lives in Casper, ended up in the hospital with back surgery and couldn't make it to the rodeo. And of course his family didn't want to come without him. So, since I had taken such good care of Mr. Bellows' mother, who lives here in Cheyenne, when she was in the hospital, and I'd mentioned to him that I was looking for a place to house our committee, he phoned and offered me his suite. And, get this, since he'd paid for it in advance, he's not charging us a dime!"

Dina's jaw dropped. "You're kidding! This place is magnificent. The cost per night must be astronomical!"

"I'm sure he's writing it off on his taxes as a public service donation."

"Even so, that was really nice of him," Burgandi inserted.

Motioning for them to follow, Celeste began climbing the stairs. "He said we should enjoy ourselves, that he considered it his privilege to help us out."

The suite Mr. Bellows had reserved took their breath away as they entered it. It was comprised of two completely autonomous rooms, joined by a common door.

"This is the Francis E. Warren Room," Celeste explained, lowering her briefcases onto the desk. "That other door leads to the Clara Warren Room. You two will be staying there. Since this is the larger room, there is plenty of space for four of us in here."

Dina couldn't help but gasp as the three of them stepped into the Clara Warren Room. With its ceiling-high windows, authentic rose-encrusted Victorian wallpaper, and its king-sized wicker and leather sleigh bed, it was truly one of the most richly decorated and feminine rooms she had ever seen.

Celeste scurried about the room, lowering the blinds, plumping bed pillows, and checking the thermostat. "We're due at the Synergy Café in an hour. Maybe you'd like to freshen up and then rest until the others are ready." She moved quickly to the door leading into the adjoining suite. "I hope you don't mind but, since we hadn't planned to officially start our meetings until tomorrow, I've scheduled several of our volunteer public service assignments for this evening."

"That's fine with me. What will Burgandi and I be doing?"

Celeste frowned. "The list is in one of my cases, but don't worry about it," she added with a smile. "Trust me, whichever task I've assigned you will be fun. I'll be delivering you to your location and picking you up after you're finished."

Since all of the members of the planning committee already knew one another, they had a great time visiting over lunch as they renewed old friendships and caught up on the four months since they'd last seen one another. Knowing most of the restaurants would be overflowing with rodeo patrons during the dinner hour, the six had opted to have pizza delivered to their room. By five thirty they had eaten, freshened up, changed clothes, and were on their way to their first assignment.

Barbara and Tracy were the first two to be dropped off. Their assignment was handing out brochures at the kiosk in the Frontier Mall.

"You still haven't said where the two of us are going," Dina reminded Celeste as the minivan exited the mall parking lot.

Celeste grinned at Dina's image in the rearview mirror. "I'm keeping it a surprise until we get there."

Kitty was the next one to exit the van. Her assignment was at the Aspenwind Assisted Living Community on College Drive. "The head nurse is expecting you. I'll come back and help you as soon as I deliver Dina and Burgandi," Celeste told her, handing her a fancy pink tote with the words NURSING IS MY BAG embroidered on its side. "Take this with you. I told them we'd be showing a video on the importance of geriatric exercise."

Though Kitty seemed a little apprehensive about working alone until Celeste returned, she waved and offered a faint smile.

"You're next. We'll be there in less than ten minutes."

Dina and Burgandi exchanged glances then settled back in

three

The sign straight ahead read FRONTIER PARK—HOME OF THE CHEYENNE RODEO.

Seeming to sense Dina's fear, Burgandi grabbed her arm. "It's okay, honey. Maybe—"

But before she could finish her sentence Celeste blurted out, with all the pride of a newly proclaimed Miss America, "We're here! You two are going to have the privilege of working in one of the famous Justin Sportsmedicine Team mobile centers. Aren't you excited?"

Excited was definitely not the word to explain how Dina felt at that moment.

Celeste beamed. "Normally, the only persons allowed to work on the Justin team are those who have been prequalified and officially authorized. But when I explained the kind of work you two do, and the world of experience you've had in your trauma units, they were eager to have you serve." She showed the man at the gate some sort of pass, then pulled on through and came to a stop near a big, shiny red gooseneck-trailer that had to be thirty-five or forty feet long. "I'll try to be back by ten o'clock. Dr. Pratt, the doctor in charge, is expecting you."

Just the thought of seeing a cowboy risk his life by participating in something so dangerous, then expecting others to volunteer to help put him back together again, made Dina want to turn and flee on foot. However, rather than make a scene, she forced herself to calm down. It was apparent Celeste thought she was doing them a favor when she had assigned her and Burgandi to work as part of the Justin team. After all the trouble the woman had gone to, she certainly didn't want to appear ungrateful. Celeste had been nothing but kind to her.

Burgandi grabbed the handle and pulled open the door. "I'll stay, but Dina's not much of a rodeo person. Maybe it would be best if she went back and spent the evening working with you and Kitty."

Dina hurriedly slipped out of her seat to join her. "No, it's fine, Burgandi, honest. I'll stay with you." Then forcing a smile, she turned to Celeste. "We'll see you about ten."

As Celeste drove off, Burgandi lodged her hands on her hips. "Why'd you tell her you'd stay?"

Dina rolled her eyes. "Because I didn't want to look like a baby. I'm a professional. It's about time I decided to act like one. But don't expect me to set foot outside of this trailer. The only cowboys I plan to see are the ones who need medical assistance, and I'm not too crazy about seeing them."

Burgandi followed Dina as she made her way up the steps of the trailer. "Yes, ma'am, whatever you say."

"You must be Dina and Burgandi," the man who greeted them at the door said as they entered the trailer. "Sure glad you're scheduled to be here tonight. Somehow we ended up shorthanded. In addition to one of our doctor's wives going into labor, there was a twelve-car pileup out on I-80. Two of our nurses are stuck out there. I understand you're trauma nurses and you've both had some training in physical therapy."

"Yes, that's true, but Dina is far more qualified than I am." After a quick glance in Dina's direction, Burgandi gave the man a smile. "I live in a small town in southwestern Nebraska, but she works in a large hospital in Omaha and treats many more injuries than I do. We're both glad to be here. Just tell us what to do."

To Dina's surprise, meeting and working with the medical staff on board the mobile unit turned out to be a real treat. She had assumed the doctors were local doctors who volunteered each time the rodeo came to their city. But, instead, these were people who, many times a year, traveled from one rodeo to another, giving as much of their time and professional expertise as they could, because of their love of the sport.

Fortunately, other than a couple of possible concussions and a broken wrist, most of the injuries they treated during the evening were minor, with most only requiring some taping up. With her father being involved in rodeo as long as he had, Dina, much to the surprise of the doctors, was well versed in the proper taping technique and wrapping of rodeo injuries.

"Hey, that rookie bull rider Wayne Warner is up next," Dr. Pratt told them as he finished up on their latest patient. "You girls ought to go watch him."

Dina shook her head. "Let someone else go. I'll stay here."

The man shrugged. "Suit yourself, but right after Wayne rides, Billy Bob is the next one up. You sure don't want to miss him. He's the main reason some of these fans come. He's had a terrific week. I wouldn't be one bit surprised if he didn't break his own record tonight."

"He's a bull rider?" Burgandi asked, as if considering his offer.

Dr. Pratt reared back with a laugh. "You haven't heard of Billy Bob? Oh, yeah, he rides bulls, the meaner the better for that man. I hear he's drawn a mean one tonight. Between him and that bull they may score as high as ninety. Maybe even higher."

Though the evening was warm, Dina wrapped her arms about herself and felt a sudden chill as vivid pictures of her father flying off that bull's back and onto the dirt beneath the huge animal's hooves filled her mind.

"Do you care if I go, Dina?" she vaguely heard Burgandi ask.

"No—go, if you want. It's fine. I–I'll stay."

Later, as she applied tape to a sprained wrist for one of the bareback contestants, Dina could hear the announcer's voice and the roar of the crowd. *Billy Bob*, she thought to herself. *Stupid man. He might be a hero today, but tomorrow he may be wishing he'd never even heard of rodeo. One fall, one misplaced step, one moment of hesitation and his career could be over.*

After she'd finished taping the man's wrist she busied herself by checking out the many nooks and crannies of the well-equipped mobile unit. It surprised her to find they had not only an intermittent compression unit, but a number of TENS units—nerve stimulation devices used to relieve pain—as well as any kind of first aid supply they would ever need. Once the two men Dr. Pratt had mentioned had finished their rides, Burgandi returned, all excited about the way the one called Billy Bob had stayed on his bull for the full eight seconds.

"You should have seen him, Dina. He was amazing! I've never seen anyone like him. He—"

Dina lifted her hand to silence her. "No more, please. I don't even want to hear about it, okay?"

Burgandi raised her shoulders in a shrug. "Okay, if you say so. Now, tell me what you've been doing while I was gone."

Since only a couple minor injuries happened after Billy Bob's ride, and the other members of the team were taking care of those contestants, Dina and Burgandi decided to wait outside the trailer, enjoying the night's breeze until Celeste arrived.

"How'd it go?" Celeste asked as Burgandi slid open the back door and the two climbed in. "Did Billy Bob have a good ride?"

Dina flinched at the sound of his name. *Billy Bob! Is that all people around here think about?*

"He was wonderful!" Burgandi responded immediately, sounding awestruck. Then glancing at Dina, she added less exuberantly, "Strange, but wonderful."

Celeste shifted slightly in her seat. "Now that we all know what we're supposed to do, I thought we would each take on the same assignment tomorrow night."

Dina couldn't believe what she was hearing.

"I'm hoping both Channel 5 and KLWY Fox will show up, someone from the newspaper, as well. I figured, if we got one evening under our belts, we'd be better prepared in case they wanted to interview us." She twisted in her seat to glance back at Dina and Burgandi. "Your assignment probably has the best opportunity for coverage. Around here, rodeo is always top news. You don't mind doing it again, do you?"

Dina and Burgandi raised their brows at one another. "No, I guess not," Dina said slowly, her response lacking proper enthusiasm. But, knowing it was for a good cause, she added a smile. "They really seemed to appreciate our help."

Celeste grinned at her in the rearview mirror. "Good. I knew I could count on you. Our meeting in the morning will start at eight. It looks like tomorrow is going to be a very long day. I hated for our first meeting to be on a Sunday, but I was trying to schedule things so you wouldn't have to be away from your jobs any longer than necessary. I know several of you normally attend church. Maybe, while you're getting ready in the morning, you can find a good preacher on TV."

❧

It was nearly three thirty the next afternoon before the nurses got away from their meeting at the bed-and-breakfast, and a few minutes past five before they returned from having a nice dinner at Celeste's favorite Mexican restaurant.

"I know I'm pushing you, but let's plan to leave here in no more than thirty minutes," she told the group as they entered their rooms. "Since this is the last night of the rodeo, the traffic is going to be heavier than usual. Oh, and you might want to wear something with a Western flair if you have it, in case you're interviewed."

"I guess you could call my blue jeans 'Western,'" Dina said in a hushed voice as she and Burgandi stepped through the adjoining door and into their room. "I'm fresh out of Western-cut, plaid, gripper-fastener shirts with saddle-stitching."

Burgandi gave her head a shake. "Aw, come on, Dina. Give Celeste a break. She's doing her best. You have to admit we did get a lot accomplished at our meeting today. Celeste is a good organizer."

Dina kicked off her shoes and stretched out full-length across the bed, clasping her hands behind her head. "I know and, even though I don't sound like it, I appreciate her efforts. It was really rude of me to make that comment, and I apologize, but this rodeo thing is getting to me. The whole town is rodeo crazy. I've never seen anything like it."

"They don't call the Cheyenne rodeo the daddy of all rodeos for nothing. I'm sure it deserves that name," Burgandi countered with a glance at the clock on the nightstand. "I hate to rush you but. . ."

Dina pulled herself into a sitting position. "I know. I'm moving."

"Wish I would have known how to reach you," Dr. Pratt told the two as they entered the Justin trailer. "You wouldn't have had to come. More volunteers showed up tonight than we could possibly use. Probably because this is the night the big winners are announced."

Burgandi wrinkled up her face at the news. "Our driver just let us off at the gate, and she won't be back after us for several hours."

He gave her a wink. "Well, lucky you. I guess that means

you two can go out into the arena and watch the show."

She brightened. "Really?"

"Sure, go out there and introduce yourselves to any of the men wearing a Justin shirt. He'll find you a good place to sit. Should be a great night. I heard Billy Bob drew Gray Ghost again. That bull is one of the meanest around. Other than Billy Bob, no one has been able to stay on that monster for more than a few seconds. Who knows? He may be the man to do it again!"

Dina turned to face the doctor. "If you don't mind, I'd rather stay here. I–I'm not interested in rodeo. Let someone else go in my place."

"Suit yourself. I can always use the company. Unless things go crazy out there and someone needs our services, it gets pretty boring in here just sitting around waiting for something to happen." He flashed a toothy grin before hastening to add, "Which is good, of course. The fewer people injured, the better."

With her expression displaying disappointment, Burgandi took hold of Dina's hand. "You might enjoy watching. You don't even want to give it a try?"

Dina gave her an emphatic, "No, I'm sorry, but I'm not going out there. You know how I feel about rodeos, especially bull riding!"

"Yes, sweetie, I do know, and I know how you feel about your dad. But not all cowboys are like him. Come and watch a couple of the events, then you can come back to the trailer when it's time for the bull riding, okay? I sure hate having to sit by myself again."

Dina never liked disappointing anyone, especially Burgandi, but what her friend was asking was too much. There was no way she was going into that arena and watch grown men, most who had families who loved them, pay their hard-earned dollars as entry fees then put their lives on the line, all because of the possibility of winning a little extra money and basking in a few minutes of glory. Maybe not every rodeo cowboy ended up like her dad, but some did. "I'm sorry, Burgandi. I can't. I just can't."

Burgandi gave her shoulder an affectionate squeeze. "Oh, honey, I understand. Forgive me. It was cruel of me to even ask."

Swallowing at her emotions, Dina forced a smile. "No harm done, but I don't want my hang-ups to keep you from enjoying yourself. Go on. You won't be alone. You'll be sitting with some of the other Justin volunteers."

Burgandi stood gazing at her for a long moment. "You sure? You don't mind?"

"Absolutely sure. Besides, we don't want Dr. Pratt getting lonely, and one of us has to stay in case any of the media show up and want an interview. After all the trouble she's gone to, Celeste would have a fit if we missed out on that." She reached out and gave Burgandi a little shove toward the door. "Have fun, but don't flirt with too many of those cute cowboys, you hear?"

Burgandi giggled. "I'll try to control myself, but some of those guys look pretty tempting in their worn jeans and cowboy hats." She headed for the door. "I promise I'll come back right after Billy Bob rides."

"No hurry. Don't worry about it." Dina followed her to the door, then stood watching until she disappeared into the crowd.

"Sure you don't want to go?" Dr. Pratt asked as he walked toward her, holding a box of Ace bandages.

"Thank you, but no. I–I'd rather stay here." She took the box from his hands and placed it in the cabinet where, she'd learned the night before, the bandages were stored.

Other than some minor injuries to a few calf ropers, a

dislocated shoulder, and a badly twisted knee, very few came into the trailer for help. Dina felt good when Dr. Pratt asked her to assist instead of a couple of the regular volunteers who had also decided to remain in the trailer. He was a nice man who loved rodeo and, she found out as they conversed between patients, had been volunteering his expertise as part of the Justin medical team for the past ten years, often traveling great distances at his own personal expense to assist at his favorite rodeos.

Burgandi came back to check on her before the second-round bull-riding event started, all excited about the way Billy Bob's first ride of the evening had gone, though Dina had little interest in what she was saying.

"Heads up!" Dr. Ryan called out as he rushed through the door and hurried to one of the open beds in the trailer. "Wayne hit the dust big-time—probably got a monster of a concussion. The team is bringing him in now."

Dina pressed herself against the wall as they entered and carried the man on a gurney past her. "Too bad, folks," she heard the announcer's voice boom through the open door. "Hopefully, Wayne was only stunned and will be back soon. Up next is the man you've all been waiting for. One of your favorites! Bil—ly Bo—b!" he drawled dramatically as the crowd went wild with applause and shouting. "And he'll be riding one of the roughest, toughest, meanest bulls around. The bull that, three times, has deprived Billy Bob of his highest wins! Grraa—ay Ghoo—st! Who'll be the winner tonight? Our mysterious Bil—ly Bo—b? Or Grraa—ay Ghoo—st? Give Billy Bob a big Cheyenne Rodeo cheer, folks!"

Dr. Pratt let out a, "Yee haw! I gotta go watch that boy ride this time." Then turning to Dina he asked, "Sure you don't want to go?"

She shook her head. "Thanks for asking, but no."

"I'll be back as quick as his ride is over."

As soon as he was out the door, Dina moved toward Dr. Ryan to see if she could be of any assistance.

❧

Billy Bob positioned himself along the top of the chute and watched as the big bull snorted and pawed his way along the narrow-railed wall toward the gate. He'd faced hundreds of bulls since he had started bull riding, but none as fierce as this one. In his opinion, Gray Ghost was the meanest, most cantankerous bull on the circuit. You never knew what he was going to do. Sometimes he came out of the chute, his head held low, his nostrils flaring, his eyes filled with fire, and headed straight toward the center of the arena before he began to kick and leap in the wild, unbridled dance for which he had become famous. No bull could kick as hard and leap as high as Gray Ghost. Other times, he'd start his leap-and-pivot routine the moment the gate opened, as if trying to crush his rider's shoulder or legs against the steel posts, dislodging him and causing great pain before the seconds had even begun to tick away.

But the thing that sent fear into the hearts of most of those who had been unfortunate enough to draw his name was the way Gray Ghost was able to defeat most riders with what his dedicated fans had begun to call his Tornado Twist. But Billy Bob had not only experienced that tornado twist and been defeated by it, he'd studied it by watching countless hours of videotape taken by other cowboys, of Gray Ghost in action, and he was ready for him. Though that bull had a mind of his own, and you never knew how he'd come out of the chute, he did have definite patterns, and if a rider could anticipate those patterns and work them to his advantage he'd have a far better chance for a winning ride.

Take your time, Billy Bob told himself, striving to be oblivious to the yelling of the crowd as he straddled the top rail and looked down at the beast he'd come to know so well. *Forget about the noise. There's no reason to hurry. This is our time together. It's Gray Ghost and me, just the two of us. Put everything else out of your mind. Concentrate on the bull. What is this beast thinking? Can he smell me? Does he know who I am? Does he remember me as the man who, several times, has stayed on his back for a full eight seconds and vowed to keep riding him until he scores over ninety?*

Almost as if the bull had read his mind, Gray Ghost reared back his head and for one brief second their eyes met. And in those eyes, Billy Bob could see a fierce determination, a doggedness, a resolve he had never before seen in a bull's eyes. It was as if Gray Ghost did remember and that his goal was to put an end to this man who dared to attempt to again ride on his back for eight seconds. And, for just the tiniest of moments, sweat poured from Billy Bob's forehead and dripped from his chin as he felt a trace of fear. He wiped at the sweat with his sleeve, leaving smudges of white and red face paint.

The fear he felt was not the fear any normal person would feel at being so close to such a powerful animal, but downright palpable fear—fear that he could taste and the feeling scared him. But, not about to let that bull rob him of the win and score he hungered for, he shook the feeling off and glared back, narrowing his eyes menacingly as he leaned closer to that massive head and the long horns that could tear a man apart. He had to let that bull know who was in charge. With the pang of fear behind him, now nothing more than an insignificant blip in his memory, he reached out, grabbed hold of a single horn, and gave it a yank, releasing it quickly, as the giant creature lunged upward in anger. Billy Bob gave Gray Ghost a grin of satisfaction. He'd shown him who was boss. All he felt now was the rush of adrenalin flowing through his veins as he sensed a win was in the making. After lifting his hat high above his head and waving it while smiling at the crowd, with the help of the chute workers, he lowered himself onto Gray Ghost's broad back, quickly slipping his hand, palm-up, into the braided leather loop of his favorite bull rope to stabilize himself.

"Watch him, Billy Bob!" one of the chute workers shouted above the roar of the crowd. "This one's dangerous!"

How well he knew. Though the bull was bucking and thrashing to the right and to the left within the confines of what little space the chute allowed him, Billy Bob took his time, making sure his leather glove was tied securely around his wrist before wrapping the rope around his hand. One error and it could be all over. When satisfied everything was as he wanted, he lifted his hand high over his head and yelled out, "Let 'er go!"

As keyed up as Gray Ghost had been while in the chute, Billy Bob fully expected him to plow out at full speed, kick and spin a few times, then go into his tornado twist. The bull had other ideas and thrust his body against one of the steel posts as he exited the chute, momentarily crushing Billy Bob's leg between the unyielding post and the bull's two-thousand-pound body, but Billy Bob barely noticed the pain. Pain went with bull riding. He'd learned long ago to ignore even the worst of pain and not allow it to rob him of his goal.

Gray Ghost zigzagged his way to the center of the arena, leaping what seemed to be straight up into the air, his hind legs flying upward and outward like an unsecured sail in a massive ocean storm. He lunged his body close to the ground, as if renewing his strength from some unseen power source. Then, using his strong legs to propel himself even higher, he thrust, kicked, and twisted, his horns seeming to be in every direction at once.

Despite Gray Ghost's sudden release of fury, Billy Bob held

on, his mind concentrating on the points he intended to make as he mentally checked the position of his legs and feet, the placement of his body on the bull's back, the reach of his hand above his head. Gray Ghost was doing his part to score as many of his allotted fifty points as possible. Billy Bob had to do his part to score his fifty. Bull and man, though enemies, were a team. They had to make it into the nineties. Nothing less would be acceptable.

Finally, after what seemed like an interminable amount of time, the buzzer sounded.

❧

"Well, there goes the buzzer," Dina told the team with an indifferent shrug as they continued to work on Wayne. "I guess that means old Billy Bob stayed on the bull's back the full eight seconds. Good for him." Her tone was mocking. "I hope he's happy."

Dr. Ryan nodded toward the door. "Leave it open so we can hear how many points he scored."

She nodded then hurried to the scrub area to wash and sanitize her hands again before returning to the table.

"What a ride," a voice boomed over the loudspeaker. "That had to be one of Billy Bob's best rides. Folks, that boy is taking the rodeo world by storm. I fully expect we'll be seeing him in Las Vegas."

"That's where the finalists from all the rodeos go. The top rodeo in the country," Dr. Ryan explained. "Dr. Pratt and I always try to make it to that one."

❧

Billy Bob smiled victoriously as he waved at the crowd. He and Gray Ghost had made it to the eight seconds, but apparently the big, angry bull didn't care. As two rodeo clowns came running toward them to make sure Billy Bob made a safe dismount, the bull changed directions, throwing him off balance. He leaned toward the opposite side, hoping to compensate, but Gray Ghost changed his plans again and immediately twisted in an unexpected direction. Rather than be thrown, Billy Bob leaped off the bull's back, hoping to land on his feet and make a quick exit, but his plans went awry and he found himself dangling at the enormous bull's side, his hand helplessly caught in the rope.

❧

Everyone in the Justin trailer snapped to attention when suddenly the announcer screamed into the microphone, "No! Trouble! Trouble! Trouble! His hand is caught in the bull rope! Clowns, help him! Get him out of there! Help that man before he's dragged to death!"

Then silence.

No applause.

No yelling.

No whistling.

Absolute silence.

Dina's heart pounded wildly as she and the others listened, waiting for news of what was happening out on the field.

"Oh, folks," the announcer continued, his voice high and shrill from excitement. "I can't believe it. It looks like Gray Ghost is out to put an end to our Billy Bob. If those clowns don't get in there soon and cut that rope. . ."

Dr. Ryan pounded his hands on a nearby table. "Come on, clowns! Get in there! Hurry!"

❧

Billy Bob couldn't believe what was happening. One moment his feet were hitting the ground. The next, he felt as if he were flying as his body was powerfully thrust into the air by Gray Ghost's erratic kicking and bucking movements.

And the pain, oh the pain, as his arm and shoulder bore the full brunt of his weight as his body hurled into the air then crashed to the ground. With his head bouncing and rebounding off of the bull's side, he was only vaguely aware of the clowns reaching and grabbing at the rope as Gray Ghost continued to move and grind, blocking their way to his prey. He tried in vain to reach out for the rope, but his strength was nearly gone and he was getting dizzy, light-headed, and—

❧

"Whew, they've done it!" the emcee announced with great relief. "He's loose—and he's on the ground, but he doesn't look good!" A hush remained over the audience, until from somewhere in the stands, a slight applause erupted, then more followed. Soon everyone present was applauding. "That's the Justin Sportsmedicine Team putting Billy Bob onto that stretcher," the man boomed.

"Good work, boys!" The announcer heaved a heavy sigh and sounded greatly relieved. "What would we do without our bull-fighting clowns? These men risk their lives night after night to save others. What an unselfish group of men." He paused, as if so caught up in the scene playing out before him, he found it hard to express himself. "Billy Bob is young," he finally managed to say, "and he's strong. We'll have to pray that Gray Ghost didn't put an end to Billy Bob's bull-riding days."

Dr. Ryan gave his head a sad shake before turning to Dina and nodding toward the open bed next to Wayne. "Stand by, Dina. I'm sure Dr. Pratt is going to need all the help he can get. Too many things are happening too fast. First Wayne, now Billy Bob."

When Dr. Pratt rushed into the trailer, shouting out instructions to the men who carried the second gurney, Dina let out a shriek of surprise. She had expected to see a cowboy, a typical bull rider dressed in denim and leather chaps, but the injured man looked like one of the clowns. His red shirt was dotted with big yellow polka dots and he was wearing clown makeup! Surely this wasn't the famous Billy Bob. Had a clown been injured, too, while trying to save the man? If so, why hadn't the announcer mentioned it?

Dr. Pratt nodded toward the Justin team carrying the gurney. "Good job. Thanks, men." Then, turning toward Dina and the others who were ready to assist, he added as he leaned over the man, "You wouldn't believe how that bull threw him around. He took a lot of punishment. It looked like old Gray Ghost was determined to do him in. I'm concerned about his leg, but it's his arm and shoulder I'm worried about most," he said in a hushed tone, lifting his face toward Dina.

"He's fortunate his injuries weren't any worse."

"Come on, man," the doctor said, lifting first one of the man's eyelids and then the other as he shone a light in his face. "Come on, Billy Bob. You can't let Gray Ghost win."

Dina's jaw dropped. "That's Billy Bob?"

He nodded. "Yeah, what's left of him."

"He's a clown?"

"No, even though he looks like one. Nobody knows why he wears these silly shirts and that makeup. We've never seen him without it. He had a beautiful ride but as he tried to dismount, somehow his hand got tangled in the bull rope and that beast dragged him around the arena, kicking and throwing him like he was a rag doll. Then, when they finally got him loose, Gray Ghost turned and tried to trample him. For a second there, I thought it was the end of Billy Bob."

Dina reached for a tissue, intending, for cleanliness' sake, to remove the man's makeup, but Dr. Pratt hurriedly stuck out his hand to stop her. "No, don't! He left emphatic orders with all of us, if he were ever to be unconscious or impaired in any way we were not to remove his makeup. Why, we don't know. He never told us. But we all respect him and his wishes. Leave it on."

"But it would be—"

The man shook his head. "Leave it, Dina. If Billy Bob wants it left on, that's the way it's going to be." Then in a whisper, he added, "I'm sure they'll take it off at the hospital but for now we'll abide by his wishes."

She withdrew her hand then stood staring at the bull rider's face. Even though his forehead was painted a chalky white, his eyelids and the area around his eyes, a brilliant blue, his shaggy eyebrows, outlined in red, something about him looked familiar. She shrugged. Maybe she'd seen him on the news. "I've never seen a shirt with that many colorful polka dots," she said, her gaze still fixed on him. "Why would a guy go to all the trouble to wear makeup and a silly-looking shirt just to ride a bull?"

The doctor shrugged. "Who knows? Some guys carry a rabbit's foot, some throw salt over their shoulder before a ride, some do even more ridiculous things to bring them luck."

She huffed. "Luck? The luckiest thing that could happen would be if they decided to give up bull riding and take up a less life-threatening form of recreation. Riding a bull does nothing but invite disaster."

"You're right about that, but I have to admit I enjoy watching them do it."

"Have you ever seen Billy Bob ride?" one of the team members asked her.

"No, and I wouldn't want to. Billy Bob, or any other bull rider."

Dr. Pratt let out a sigh of relief as a long, low groan sounded from his patient. "I knew Billy Bob was too tough to give up that easily. It may be a long time before he's able to compete again, but I have a feeling old Gray Ghost and Billy Bob will be meeting again someday."

Dina gasped as her hand went to her chest. "You honestly

think he'll want to ride again? After that bull nearly killed him?"

Dr. Pratt snorted. "Sure he will. Bull riders are a whole other breed of men. Once a bull rider, always a bull rider. They never quit. It's in their blood."

Though she knew the doctor couldn't see her, Dina rolled her eyes. Then, rather than have a verbal sparring match with Dr. Pratt, who obviously loved the sport of bull riding, said to herself, *They never quit—unless a bull takes that option away from them and they end up in a wheelchair like my dad. Then it's too late.*

He removed an instrument from the tray on the table and began to cut away at the injured man's sleeve. After one of the other team members removed Billy Bob's chaps, Dr. Pratt carefully cut away his left pant leg.

"Augghh. What happened?" the man on the table asked in a distorted whisper as his eyes opened in a narrow slit. Then, forcing them wider, he squinted and blinked at the doctor, as if trying to focus in on him. "Did any of the clowns get hurt?"

Dina was surprised the man's first words were of concern for the clowns. He didn't even ask about his own injuries.

"Other than a few scratches and scrapes, the clowns are fine." Dr. Pratt nodded toward Dina. "Alert the ambulance crew. We need to get this man to the Cheyenne Regional Medical Center."

Dina did as she was told then watched the ambulance crew as they quickly entered and snapped into action.

"I'd go with him but. . ." Dr. Pratt motioned toward Dr. Ryan who was still working with the other bull rider. "I'd better stay here, in case anyone else is injured. Would you mind going with him, Dina? I'm sure one of the officers at the hospital will see that you get back to where you're staying when you're ready. I'd feel better if, considering your experience with your trauma unit, you rode along."

She really didn't want to go with him. He'd brought his injuries on himself. But her caring side, the side that had made her want to be a nurse in the first place, kicked in and forced her to say yes.

"I got here as soon as I could!" a breathless voice said. Dina turned as wide-eyed Burgandi rushed into the trailer. "They made everyone stay in their places until the EMTs got Billy Bob off the field. How is he?"

"Not good, but he's conscious. They're taking him to the hospital. Dr. Pratt wants me to ride along with him."

Burgandi's expression showed concern. "Are you up to it? I could go."

"Thanks, but I'll go. I'll meet you back at the bed-and-breakfast. Dr. Pratt said one of the officers would bring me." Dina took her purse from the cabinet where she'd placed it then followed the EMTs to the ambulance. Once she'd settled herself inside and had a chance to lean closer to her patient, she had to clamp her hand over her mouth to keep from shouting out that the man looked so much like Will, the man who had rescued her when she ran out of gas. The resemblance was uncanny. Of course with the makeup on, she couldn't be sure about his face, but that beard? She'd recognize it anywhere. But what would Will be doing riding bulls at a rodeo? And if it were Will, why would everyone be calling him Billy Bob? The whole idea was ludicrous.

Ludicrous or not, she had to ask. "I know this sounds strange, and I hate to ask since you're in so much pain, but—isn't your real name Will?"

A sudden look of panic came over his face. "Don't tell, please don't tell."

"That you're Will?"

"Yes. Don't want anyone to know. Important to me."

Though her curiosity was trying to get the better of her,

she wasn't about to ask why. She was nothing more to him than the nurse who was accompanying him to the hospital. What he said or did was of his own choosing. "Then I won't say a word. It's none of my business anyway."

"Was Dr. Pratt—telling me—the truth?" he asked as Dina turned her full attention to checking his vitals.

She frowned. "About your injuries?" She never liked discussing a patient's injuries with them, not even a famous bull rider's. That was the doctor's area.

He opened his eyes a slit. "No. The clowns."

"You mean about none of them being hurt?"

His only response was a slight nod.

"None, as far as I know. I'm sure if any of them had sustained serious injuries, we would have been told about it."

After a nearly undetectable sigh, he closed his eyes. "Good. I was worried about them."

His concern about their well-being touched her heart, especially in light of his own injuries. Though she rarely touched a patient except in the line of duty, she felt compelled to give his good shoulder a comforting pat. "And I'm sure they're worried about you."

They arrived at the hospital much sooner than she'd expected. "The hospital is going to expect some means of identification, you know," she told him with concern.

"Insurance card." With his good hand, he gestured toward his left side. "Back pocket."

Dina waited until they had rolled him inside and were ready to transfer him to an examination table then asked one of the technicians to take it out of his pocket.

Knowing from experience how important it was for the trauma crew to have as much information about a patient's injuries as possible, she quickly gave them a rundown of how the bull had tried to crush his leg as they came out of the chute, and how his hand had gotten entangled in the rope, being sure to add Dr. Pratt's findings as well as Will's vitals since his accident had happened.

The doctor on duty thanked her then motioned to the nurse. "Get that stuff off his face. I'm surprised the Justin team didn't take it off."

Knowing he'd be none too pleased about losing his makeup, she cast a glance in Will's direction before moving to an inconspicuous place along the wall where she stood watching as the doctor resumed his examination. There really wasn't any real purpose in her staying. Her job was finished. But for some unknown reason, especially now that she knew he was really Will, she felt an obligation to be there.

"Hey, you're a pretty good-lookin' guy," the doctor told him, pulling off his latex gloves with a chuckle once he'd finished his examination and Will's makeup had been removed.

Dina was in total agreement.

"Now, cowboy, we have to get you up to Radiology. I don't like the looks of your arm or that shoulder—or your leg. Doesn't look like you'll be riding bulls for quite a while."

"But—"

The doctor held up his hand to silence him. "No buts about it, young man. I hate to say it, because I know you don't want to hear it, but you're going to need months of healing time and a lot of physical therapy to get you back to where you can tangle with bulls again." He added a snicker. "Of course my best advice would be that you forget about rodeo, except maybe as a spectator."

He turned to Dina. "Thanks for coming in with him, but you can go now."

"No, I'll stay awhile." Dina's words surprised even her. "He needs someone here with him. I'll call whoever he wants called and let them know what's happened."

"I'm sure he'd appreciate it." Lowering his voice, he continued. "I'm bringing in an orthopedic specialist. If the X-rays show what I think they will, Mr. Martin will probably end up in surgery early tomorrow." He motioned toward the bed. "Someone will be here shortly to take him to Radiology."

"Is there anyone you'd like me to call?" Dina asked, bending over him as soon as the doctor had gone. "A relative or friend maybe?"

Will opened his eyes wide then answered with a weak, "No."

She stared at him for a moment, taking careful note of his shaggy beard, his heavy eyebrows, and his wild, thick hair, but mostly his eyes. She'd thought of those eyes, those beautiful sky blue eyes, countless times since she'd visited her friend's home in southwestern Nebraska. "I still can't believe you're the man who was nice enough to try to start my car and then drove me to the Coulters' ranch."

He stared at her, his eyes almost pleading. "Promise you won't tell anyone. Please."

Dina lifted her hands in a surrender fashion. "Don't worry about it. I won't say a word. Whatever name you want to call yourself is really none of my business."

"Don't mention Nebraska."

Now she was really confused. "You don't want anyone to know you're from Nebraska?"

He moved his head in a slight bobbing motion. "Yes. Don't tell."

"Okay, I won't mention it, though I can't imagine what difference it would make. Are you sure there isn't someone you'd like me to call?"

"No!" His answer was so quick and firm it caught her off guard.

"There *has* to be someone," she told him, unable to imagine him going through this ordeal alone.

"No. No one."

Dina glanced at her watch. Her roommates had probably already gotten back to the hotel and were soaking in the hot tub. "I'd planned to stay, at least until you went to Radiology, but I guess I could stay longer, if you want me to."

"Don't want to take your time."

She sent him a gentle smile. "Don't worry about it. I'm a nurse, remember? I'm used to hospitals and working the late-night shift."

He fixed his gaze on her and almost looked as if he wanted to tell her something but wasn't sure if he should.

"What? What is it?" she asked, curious but not wanting to pry.

He hesitated then answered in a whisper so soft she couldn't be sure she'd heard him right. "You're scared? Is that what you said?"

He nodded.

"There's nothing wrong with being scared," she told him, wanting so much to console him. "You wouldn't be human if you weren't. But usually things don't turn out half as bad as we imagine they will. You have to believe you'll be fine."

What else could she say? What could she do to comfort him? Even though he was a bull rider and had no one to blame for his injuries other than himself, what she wanted to do was wrap him in her arms and tell him he would soon be back to his old self. But that would be a lie. Until the results of the X-rays were read and the severity of his injuries known, there was no way of knowing much of anything. He might recover fairly quickly, or he might end up like. . . She shuddered at the thought. *No, not like my father!* Just thinking about that possibility made her stomach quiver. Grasping his hand in hers and holding it tight, she decided to do what she should have done in the ambulance. Pray.

four

Will felt like Gray Ghost had not only mashed his leg against the chute post and dragged him about the arena by his arm, but had plopped all of his two thousand pounds right down on top of him. Every bone, muscle, and nerve ached.

Now what? Though he'd done well at the Cheyenne rodeo, his winnings wouldn't begin to cover his doctor and hospital costs. What little insurance he carried might help, and he knew he could count on the Rodeo Contestant Crisis Fund to give him some financial assistance, but those things wouldn't come close to taking care of his medical bills if his injuries were half as bad as he suspected. If he hadn't felt so rotten, he would have given his head a sad shake. He not only couldn't afford the costs his bout with Gray Ghost had caused him, he couldn't afford the time it would take to recover, not with the amount of responsibility he carried on his shoulders. His family needed him.

He glanced up when someone took hold of his hand. It was Dina. That woman had the face of an angel. He'd thought of her day and night since he'd found her stranded on that abandoned road. What was it about this beautiful person that made his head swim, his knees shake, and his heart beat like it was in a race for first place? She was beautiful, that was sure, but she was far more than that. She was a wonderful, caring person whose smile lit up the room and made his dire situation almost hopeful.

"Do you mind if I pray for you?" she asked, breaking into his thoughts. "I quite often pray for my friends and patients when they ask me to. God is the Great Physician, you know." She smiled as she gave his hand a slight squeeze. "During my time as a nurse I've seen many miracles happen when people pray."

"Sure. Thanks. I'd appreciate it." Her words excited him. He'd seen miracles, too, and was trusting God to perform a much-needed miracle for him.

He listened with rapt attention as she spoke aloud to God, asking Him to touch him, comfort him, calm his fears, lessen his pain, and be with him as he went into Radiology. He'd never had a near-stranger pray for him, and certainly never anyone as pretty, or as capable of understanding his injuries, as the woman who had come into his life in such unexpected ways. She was like an angel sent from God to not only pray for him and bring hope into the most frightening time of his life, but to encourage his faith in the God he had known since he was a child. The God in whom, at times, he'd nearly lost confidence because of the circumstances his family had found themselves in the day he turned twelve, a birthday he'd never forget.

When she finally said, "Amen," Will had to fight back tears. After all, grown men like him didn't cry.

"Do you know the Lord, Will?" she asked as he opened his eyes.

But before he could answer, two men in blue scrubs appeared with a gurney. Dina quickly tucked her long blond hair behind one ear then leaned close to his face and whispered, "You shouldn't be alone at a time like this. I'm going to stay until they're finished with you, and I'll be praying for you," before stepping back out of the way.

Within minutes, they had transferred him from the table to the gurney and, though it pained him to do so, as they rolled him out into the hallway, he turned his head for one final glimpse of Dina. He wanted to remember her beautiful face forever. Would she really stay until they'd finished with him? With all the injuries he had, it could be hours.

As he relaxed his neck, in his heart he cried out to God. *God, I've faced some scary things before but I've never been this afraid. I know I don't deserve to ask, but please bring me through this, not for my sake but for the sake of my family. I know a person isn't supposed to try to bargain with You, God, the Ruler and Creator of the universe, but, I promise, if You bring me through this, I'll do the best I can to live for You.*

❧

Dina followed the gurney into the hallway then smiled at Will as he turned his head and their eyes met. She waited in the hallway until the gurney disappeared into an elevator before going down to the main floor, stepping outside, and dialing Burgandi's number.

"Where are you? Do you have any idea what time it is?" her friend nearly shouted into the phone. "I thought one of the officers was going to bring you back."

"I'm still at the hospital. They've just taken Wi—ah, Billy Bob up to Radiology. I'm. . ." She paused, knowing her roommate was going to think she had gone bonkers. "I'm going to stay until they finish with him." Dina wanted to tell her who he was—the man who'd helped her when she'd had car trouble—but she didn't. He'd asked that she tell no one, so she wouldn't. Not even Burgandi.

"You have got to be kidding! What's wrong with you, Dina? Aren't you the woman who refused to have anything to do with a man who rode bulls? You wouldn't even go watch him ride."

She searched her heart. Why *was* she staying? Why was she helping a near-stranger? She didn't know the answers. All she knew was that she had to do it.

"I was shocked," Burgandi went on, not even stopping long enough for a breath, "when you consented to ride along in the ambulance. I never thought you'd *stay* with him!"

"I have to stay. He—he needs me." She'd no sooner said it than she realized how stupid her answer must sound to Burgandi, after all the raving and ranting she'd done about bull riders.

"He *needs* you? You don't even know the man. How could he need you?"

"I can't explain it. I just know he does, and I promised I'd stay."

"Are you forgetting about our meeting? It starts at eight. Celeste is going to sizzle if you don't make it. Your report is the first one of the morning."

"No, I haven't forgotten, but. . ." She didn't want to let Celeste down but, right now, Will and what he would be facing in the weeks, probably even months to come, were uppermost on her mind. "I'm planning on making it back in plenty of time." Again she paused. "But if, for any reason, I don't, you will explain my absence for me, won't you?"

"How can I explain something I don't understand myself? But I'm your friend. I'll do the best I can."

"Thanks, Burgandi. I knew I could count on you. Will you do me another favor? Pray for Billy Bob. He needs it."

"You got it. I love you, sweetie. Wake me up when you get back. *If* you get back."

Dina thanked her again, said good night, then hung up the phone.

"Are you the woman who came in with the man from the rodeo?" a nurse asked as she approached Dina. "He wanted me to give you this and tell you thanks for staying."

Dina took the plastic bag then said a grateful, "Thank you. Do you have any idea how long it will be before he's finished in Radiology?"

"We're pretty busy up there tonight, so I'm guessing it could be as much as a couple of hours. But you can come up and wait in the Radiology waiting room, if you like."

Dina thanked the woman then followed her. She found a comfortable-looking chair in the corner of the room and then, not sure it was any of her business, sat down to open the bag she'd received. It didn't contain much, probably because, when they ride, bull riders wanted as little as possible in their pockets. There was a single dime, an old key, and a small crumpled snapshot of a man and a young boy. That was it. Why would a grown man, especially a strong, tough one like Will, carry such insignificant items with him while riding bulls? To bring him luck maybe? And why did he feel they were important enough to make sure someone would hold on to them for him?

She picked up a magazine and then, after flipping through the pages, placed it back on the coffee table. It seemed nothing could take her mind off him. She adjusted her position several times, trying to find a comfortable way to curl up and maybe catch a little sleep, but it didn't work. No matter how tightly she closed her eyes, her thoughts kept going back to the man in Radiology.

"Oh, Dina, there you are." It was Dr. Pratt. "I don't know if the rest of the bull riders were spooked because of Wayne's and Billy Bob's injuries or what, but after you two left, it seemed every contestant ended up with injuries of one kind or another." He quickly seated himself next to her. "How is he?"

She sighed. "No news yet. He tried to put on a brave front and act like he wasn't in pain, but he was. I could see it in his eyes."

"I was surprised you were still here. I felt bad after you left, that I had asked you to ride in the ambulance, knowing how you felt about bull riding."

She gave him a sheepish grin. "I'd planned on going to our hotel as soon as they got him checked in, but I couldn't leave him. He looked so sad, and he was alone."

"I'm glad you stayed. I know you haven't been around Billy Bob long enough to get to know him but, in my opinion, he's one of the finest men I've ever met. I'm sure they took off that makeup."

She nodded. "Yes, they did. Do you have any idea why he wears it?"

"Only reason most of us could come up with was that he wanted to remain anonymous and that was his way of doing it." He freed a small chuckle. "If I didn't hold him in such high regard, I might think he's running from the law."

"It's a shame he wears it. I liked him so much better without it."

"Liked? Past tense? Does that mean you knew him before?"

Dina had been guarding her words so carefully she couldn't believe she'd goofed. "I'd met him once, briefly, under entirely different circumstances and in a different place. I hadn't realized the man I'd met and Billy Bob were one and the same. Until tonight," she hastened to add. "But his eyes were a dead giveaway. I could never forget those beautiful blue eyes." She felt herself blushing. She'd said far more than she should have.

Dr. Pratt scooted his chair closer then leaned toward her. "I don't want you to betray any confidences, but is there anything you can tell me about him? I promise anything you say will be between the two of us. I'd never do anything to hurt Billy Bob." His eyes narrowed. "Or is that his real name? I have a feeling you know."

This time Dina was extremely careful with her words before uttering them. "Actually, other than seeing his face and having a general idea of where he lives, I doubt I know any more than you do."

"Where did you meet him? You haven't said."

"I'm sorry, Dr. Pratt, but I'm afraid anything else you'd like to know will have to come from Billy Bob himself."

He gave her arm a pat then moved his chair back to its original place. "I'm sorry to have put you on the spot, but all of us who love rodeo are in awe of Billy Bob. If you just recently met him, you may not know this, but a couple of years ago he showed up on the rodeo circuit, registering himself as simply Billy Bob, no last name. No address. And where the form said state, he wrote in USA. And the craziest part? He was wearing that same makeup he was wearing tonight. Everyone loves a mystery. The fans immediately went crazy for him, partly because of the mystique that surrounded him, but mainly because he proved to be one of the best bull riders around. After a decent night, he'd collect his purse, disappear, and no one would see him 'til rodeo time the next night. Then, once that rodeo was over, we didn't see or hear from him until time for the next one. Some folks even began to call him the Rodeo Phantom, but it didn't stick. I guess they liked the name Billy Bob better. It was obvious that boy had been riding bulls for a long time, probably in competition under another name, without the clown face. He won that first big event as Billy Bob and has been winning ever since."

"I can see why the fans like him. You're right. Everyone loves a good mystery."

"Yeah, and it couldn't happen to a nicer guy. It's sure been fun watching him rise to the top. I had fully expected to see him make Las Vegas next year." His shoulders rose in a sad shrug. "But—now—after what happened tonight—who knows? His bull-riding days may be over."

As far as Dina was concerned, nothing would please her more than to hear Will say he was through with rodeo. The man had no business even entertaining the thought of ever climbing onto a bull's back again. Hopefully, the injuries he had sustained would be a wake-up call before some bull caused his death.

Dr. Pratt stood to his feet and, with a yawn, stretched his long arms first one way then the other. "Well, since you're staying, I guess I'll go. It's been a long day." After fishing around in his pocket, he handed her his card. "Call me when you find out about his surgery."

She thanked him for coming then said good-bye. She'd barely settled down in her chair again when he hurried back into the room. "Oh, yeah. I forgot something. If you get to talk to him and you want to cheer him up, tell him he and old Gray Ghost scored a 94, and he won first place in bull riding. That, and the money it'll bring him, should make him feel better."

Even though she hated bull riding, she couldn't help but be pleased. She knew enough from her father's rodeo days to know a 94 was nearly unachievable. If his ride on Gray Ghost had to be his last ride ever, it would be of some comfort to know he'd gone out at the peak of his career. She could hardly wait to tell him.

Nearly an hour later, the nurse who had brought her up to the waiting room appeared. "We're finished. They'll be taking him to his room in a few minutes. Dr. Grimes will be in shortly to discuss their findings with you. After you've met with him, I'll take you to Mr. Martin's room."

It seemed an eternity before Dr. Grimes joined her. She couldn't believe how fidgety she had become waiting for him.

"I'm Dr. Grimes, and you're. . ."

"Dina. Dina Spark."

"I wish I had better news, Miss Spark, but Mr. Martin took quite a beating by that bull." He pulled a chair up in front of her and sat down. "I've discussed our findings on the phone with Dr. Farha, an excellent Denver orthopedic surgeon who is part of the Justin team of volunteer doctors. He's flying into Cheyenne in the morning. We've scheduled Mr. Martin's surgery for two o'clock tomorrow afternoon."

"Dr. Farha is coming all the way from Denver?"

"Yes. As a matter of fact, he called us. Being a part of the Justin team, he was already well aware of what had happened and was eager to come. The good news is your friend's leg isn't as bad as we'd first feared. Our main concern is the shoulder, and the way his arm was twisted while bearing Mr. Martin's weight as that bull dragged him around the field. I'd try to better explain the extent of his injuries, but it's usually hard for a lay person to understand."

"I'm a trauma nurse, Dr. Grimes. I'd appreciate anything you can tell me."

"Oh? In that case, there are a few things you should know." He went on to explain the various arthroscopic surgery procedures Dr. Farha had recommended with hopes that their use would help shorten Will's recovery time. "But don't worry. Dr. Farha is one of the best arthroscopic surgeons around. He'll put Mr. Martin back together. That young man should be able to walk on his leg by the end of the week, but his shoulder and arm are going to take time to heal, and he'll have to go through weeks of physical therapy. But who knows? He may be back riding bulls before we know it."

Dr. Grimes might have thought his last words would cheer her up, but they didn't. Be back riding bulls? She hoped Will wouldn't be that stupid.

"Maybe you'd better go on home and come back in the morning. "

"I have to go to him," she told him adamantly. "I promised."

He stood then reached out and shook her hand. "Then, by

all means, Miss Spark, go. But you'd better hurry. We'll soon be giving him something to make him sleep. We want him to be well rested for tomorrow."

Will was asleep when she entered his room, or at least that was the way it appeared. Though he was a big man, with muscles any body builder would be proud to claim, he looked as helpless as a premature newborn as he lay there. Dina approached his bed cautiously and stood gazing at him. *Why would any man go to all the trouble to put on makeup to ride a bull? Unless he had something to hide.*

She startled when he opened his eyes and gazed up at her.

"I—I didn't think you'd stay." He groaned as he attempted to shift his arm. "Thanks."

"You're welcome." She held up the little bag. "The nurse said you told her to give this to me. I'll keep it for you until after you've had surgery if you like."

He fingered his beard with his good hand. "I wish they would have left my makeup on."

She smiled at his words. "Only women are allowed to wear makeup in hospitals. But don't worry about it. I doubt anyone will recognize you without it, especially since you're registered here as William Martin. But if any of your fans were determined to find you they might recognize your hair and that beard. Yours is very—unique."

"You're probably right."

"You won't be riding bulls again for quite a while. I'm certainly not a barber but when I was in high school I cut my friends' hair all the time, and I used to trim my dad's hair between haircuts. They all said I had a knack for it. I could borrow a pair of scissors from one of the nurses and trim your hair quite a bit shorter if you like. You could have a barber touch it up later."

He fingered his beard with his good hand. "What about

this? I don't want it shaved but I wouldn't mind a close trim."

"I've never trimmed a man's beard before. I'll bet a male nurse would do it for you. I could ask."

He appeared to be thinking it over then nodded. "Yeah, sure. That's a good idea. Thanks." A smile quirked up the corners of his lips. "That way, for sure, no one will recognize me. I'm not even sure I'll recognize myself without this mass of hair and my beard trimmed short."

"I'll bet you'll be quite handsome." Her expression softened. She sure didn't want to talk him into anything he didn't feel like doing. "I know you're hurting, Will, but would you like me to cut it now? I might even be able to talk someone into trimming your beard right away, too. Before they give you something to make you sleep?"

"Sure, why not? Let's get it over with while I'm in the mood."

Though she wanted to ask him more about why he wore his hair and beard that way, she didn't. He was entitled to his privacy. Instead, she excused herself and hurried out of the room in search of a pair of scissors and a willing male nurse.

Within less than an hour a weary, near-stranger smiled up at her from his bed. "How do I look?" Will asked with a happy smile and more of his face showing than she'd ever seen.

"I can't get over the way cutting off your hair and trimming that shaggy beard changes you."

"For the better, I hope."

"Much better, but I have to admit I was beginning to like it the way it was."

"Maybe I should have left it."

She gave his good shoulder a pat. "Oh, no. You're—gorgeous this way."

He scrunched up his face. "Gorgeous?"

"Well, maybe not gorgeous but I can safely say you're extremely handsome. I'm. . ." She stepped back, twisting her head first one way and then the other. "I'm having a hard time realizing it's actually you."

"It's me alright. But I can tell you I'd much rather be riding on a bull's back than be in this hospital bed."

She snapped her fingers. "By the way, Dr. Pratt was here earlier. He said to tell you that you and Gray Ghost scored a 94 on your last ride."

His eyes widened. "A 94? Really? I'll have to thank Gray Ghost when I see him."

"You want to thank that bull? After what he did to you?"

"He only did what came naturally to him. He meant me no harm."

She let out a sardonic laugh. "No harm? That bull nearly killed you!"

"He didn't set out to kill me. He only did what bulls do. I agitated him by climbing on his back and spurring him. If a stranger climbed onto my back and tried to ride me like that, I'd buck them off just like he did me."

"But he dragged you around the arena!"

"Not by choice. It wasn't his fault my hand got tangled in the rope. It was mine. If I'd done things the way I was supposed to, I would have slipped off his back after the buzzer sounded, gotten out of his way, and I'd be back at the hotel in bed instead of lying here in the hospital."

"That isn't all Dr. Pratt said. He wanted you to know you were named this year's Bull Riding Champion. The big number one."

He brightened. "That's great! Wow! Being named Bull Riding Champion of the Year has been my goal ever since I started rodeoing. Too bad I wasn't there to enjoy it, but there's always next year."

She gave her head a sad shake. "What's with all you cowboys? You get hurt and then go back again and again. It's like you're challenging fate. Do you think you're invincible?"

"No, ma'am. I know I'm not invincible but I have to keep riding. Bull riding gets in your blood. It's like you're not complete unless—"

"Unless you're challenging fate, with hopes of staying on a bull's back for eight seconds and making the highest score."

"I guess you could say that, but—ah—the money is nice, too. Where else can a guy win that much?"

"But is the money worth it?" She gestured toward his battered body as it lay covered with a pristine white blanket. "Look at you! You told me you were a rancher. Who is going to do the chores and take care of your herd while you're recovering from surgery and going through the many months of healing and physical therapy you're facing?"

He let out a slow breath of air. "That's the question I've been asking myself. I don't know. My mom is pretty good at it but she can't handle it on her own. I have two brothers but one of them, Ben, lives in West Virginia. Jason is still in college in Kentucky. He's working on his Masters in biology. Teresa, my little sister, is great help around the ranch during her summer breaks from college, but there's only so much two women can do. Maybe my neighbor will help me out."

She felt like a heel for pushing him. The poor guy was facing surgery, with no idea of how he was going to come out. "You shouldn't be worrying about things like that now. It may not be as bad as it seems." Her gaze went toward the open door. "I'd better be going. The nurse will be here soon with something to make you sleep."

"My surgery is tomorrow."

"I know. I spoke with your doctor." His sad expression was almost more than she could bear. Wanting him to know she really was concerned about him and his uncertain future, she moved closer and gently placed her hand on his good arm. "I'm sure Dr. Farha will do everything he can to get you back to normal as soon as possible."

They both turned as a nurse breezed into his room. Her smile alone would have put anyone at ease. "Sorry to break into your conversation, but I've got a something that will make this man sleep like a baby."

Will puckered up his face. "It won't make me sick, will it?"

She laughed. "No, only sleepy. You'll be out before you know it."

After giving him his medication, she refilled his water glass, asked if there was anything else she could do, then disappeared as fast as she'd appeared.

"Thanks for staying. It means a lot to have you here."

"You're quite welcome. Are you sure you don't want me to call someone to come and stay with you when you come out of recovery?"

"No. No one."

"But you need someone here with you." His pitiful expression broke her heart. "If you want me to, I guess *I* could come back." The words slipped out of her mouth before she had time to think them over.

"Would you?" His eyes were pleading, almost begging.

"I have a report to give in the morning, but I'm sure I can slip away after that. I'll try to be here before they take you to Prep."

"Thanks. I'll feel better knowing you're here. You've been so kind to me. I hate to ask, but there is something else you could do for me, if you would."

"Oh, what?"

"You've seen my pickup. It's parked out behind the Super 8 on West Lincolnway. Is there any way you could get my wallet from under the seat and bring it to me?"

She couldn't keep a frown from creasing her forehead. "You left your wallet in your truck?"

"Yeah, I always keep my insurance card in my back pocket when I ride bulls—just in case—but I put a bag with everything else in it under the front seat and locked it. The truck key is in that bag the nurse gave you."

"No problem. I'll be glad to get it for you." She straightened his covers and pulled them up about his neck, not sure if she was doing it because she was a nurse and that was what she did for her patients, or if she was doing it because she felt sorry for him. Maybe both. By the time she finished, his eyes were already closed, the medication the nurse had given him already taking effect. "Sleep tight," she said in a faint whisper, leaning even closer to his ear. And then on impulse she lightly kissed his cheek.

As she backed out of the room, she took one final glance at the man in the bed. It almost looked as if he was smiling. Surely he hadn't realized she'd kissed him!

Once outside the hospital she hailed a cab. "Super 8 Motel, please."

five

Burgandi's clenched hand anchored on her hip as the two sat in their hotel room the next morning. "You have got to be kidding!"

Dina put her favorite tube of lipstick back into her purse then zipped it shut. "I promised. I can't go back on my promise. He's counting on me."

"But you barely know the man! And he's a cowboy. A bull-riding cowboy! Have you forgotten what you told me?"

"No, I haven't forgotten, but I didn't say I'd never talk to a cowboy or treat one like a human being if he needed it. I just said I'd never have anything to do with one—on a serious basis," she hastened to add. "He's merely a man facing surgery alone. Being there to encourage him is the least I can do."

"Do you have any idea how upset Celeste is going to be when she finds out you're missing this afternoon's meeting?"

"You can take notes for me."

"And you think that will appease her?"

"I guess it'll have to, because I'm going." Dina picked up her jacket and tugged it on.

"You, my friend, are a stubborn, unpredictable woman."

She reached out and gave the strap of Burgandi's shoulder bag a tug. "I know, but you love me anyway, right?"

"Yeah, I love you. What choice do I have? You're my closest friend."

They decided not to tell Celeste she was leaving until after she had given her report and, like they had expected, the woman didn't like the idea one bit. "You're a vital part of this committee, Dina," she nearly shrieked at her. "It's nice of you to offer to stay with the man, but he is not your responsibility."

"You are absolutely right," she told the woman in a soft, controlled voice. "But everyone deserves to have someone there with them when they come out of recovery. Knowing how thoughtful you are," she decided to add honestly, "I'm sure you would do exactly the same thing if you were in my place."

Celeste, apparently dazzled by Dina's compliment, gazed at her for a moment, then smiled. "Yes, I'm sure I would. Go on and go to him. We'll bring you up to speed later."

She left the hotel by noon, hoping she would make it to the hospital in time. Fortunately, Will was still in his room when she arrived, his bed propped up slightly. He smiled at her as she entered. "Thanks. I—I was afraid you wouldn't come."

"Didn't I tell you I'd be here?"

"Yes, ma'am, but even people I thought I could trust have let me down."

"Well, *I* didn't let you down." She held up his blue canvas bag. "I got it for you last night, just like I said I would." The smile that formed on his face made her late-night trip to the motel worth the effort.

"I appreciate you going to all that trouble. I'll find some way to repay you."

"No payment necessary. I was glad to do it. Did you sleep well?"

He nodded. "Yes, ma'am, but I had the strangest dream."

"About the bull?"

"No, ma'am." He gave her a sheepish grin. "I dreamed someone kissed me."

She felt a flush rise to her cheeks. "Oh?"

"I've never had a dream like that. It was—sorta nice."

Dina pulled off her jacket and draped it over a chair. "Sometimes medication causes dreams."

His grin broadened. "Maybe. I sure appreciate your being here. I'm never keen on having surgery."

"I guess that means you've had surgery before." *Probably from other rodeo injuries.*

"Yeah, simple stuff, like having my tonsils out. Nothing major like Dr. Farha is going to do."

"I thought maybe you were talking about rodeo injuries."

"Oh, I've had lots of those, but none serious enough to require surgery. I never ride without my protective vest. That helps. Mostly all I needed during those times I got hurt was a bit of taping up or a few stitches."

Again, she thought of her father. "If that's all you've had, and you're a bull rider, you're a mighty lucky man."

"I know. I thank the Lord for it every day."

"You do?"

His brows narrowed. "What? Thank the Lord?"

"Yes. I mean—do you really thank Him, or was that just a figure of speech?"

"Are you asking me if I'm a Christian?"

"I tried to ask you before, but the men with the gurney came for you and you didn't have a chance to answer me."

"Yes, ma'am, I—"

"You have got to stop calling me *ma'am*. We're friends, Will. Call me Dina."

"I like your name. It's pretty. Just like you."

She felt as if she were blushing. "So—are you a Christian?"

"Yes, ma'am—Dina—I am. I'd be afraid to ride bulls if I wasn't. I ask God to protect me before every ride and I give Him the full credit when He does."

"Does that mean, just because you know God, you think He approves of your taking ridiculously dangerous chances with the life He gave you?" She had to ask, because what he did just didn't make sense to her.

"I know riding bulls must seem stupid to you, but other than the fact that I enjoy it, I do have my reasons."

Smiling, a slightly rotund nurse came in and circled his bed. "They'll be here to take you to the surgical floor any minute now. Are we ready?"

Dina laughed to herself at the woman's use of the word *we*. As a nurse herself, she avoided asking patients, *Are we ready*? as if she were going to go into surgery and be operated on right along with them. "Could we just have a moment? I'd like to pray for him."

The nurse's smile broadened. "Of course you may. A person can never have too much prayer. I'll be right outside."

He reached out his good hand. "I was hoping you'd pray for me, 'cause I admit it. I'm scared, Dina, really scared."

She moved closer to the bed and entwined her fingers with his. It was hard to imagine big, tough Will afraid of anything. But, in his eyes, she saw fear. Fear of what, she wasn't sure. Fear of coming under the surgeon's knife? Of never being able to ride bulls again? Or losing the full use of his arm? The man before her was a man of mystery, not only to her but to everyone else. Yet, mystery or not, for some reason she couldn't understand, God had brought them together. And that was reason enough for her to be there, praying for him and holding his hand. Though she didn't feel very strong at that moment, whatever strength she had, she wanted to share with Will.

"I know you are. We're all scared when we face the unknown but God is with you, Will. You're far from alone." She tightened her grip on his hand. "I'm here, too, and I'll be here waiting when you come back from surgery."

"You'll do that for me? It'd sure mean a lot to me to have you here but didn't you say you're in town for meetings?"

The look of gratitude on his face brought tears to her eyes. "Of course I'll do it. Being here is far more important than any meeting."

"You mean it?"

"Absolutely. There's no place I'd rather be today than here with you."

He closed his eyes and swallowed hard. "Somehow—I'll find a way to repay you for all your kindnesses toward me. Not many women would give up their time to stand by someone they barely know."

"We're even. You were kind to me when you found me stranded on that road."

"I didn't begin to do for you what you've done for me." He gazed into her face. "Other than my mom, you're the most wonderful woman I've ever met." His fingers tightened around hers. "You're an angel sent from God."

She smiled down at him. "I don't know about the angel part, but I'm glad God brought us together."

"Me, too."

Bowing her head, she began to pray aloud.

She stayed by his side until they'd loaded him onto the gurney, then lingered in the doorway, watching until he disappeared out of sight. When the phone on his night table rang she hurried to answer it, hoping it would be Burgandi since she had given her the direct-dial number.

"Wow, you answered quick." It was Burgandi. "Has your cowboy gone to surgery yet?"

Dina rolled her eyes, ready to chastise her friend for her comment, then decided not to. "Yeah, they just took him."

"We caught the noon news while we were having lunch. From what the TV anchor said, I guess everyone is concerned about your Billy Bob, even those not interested in rodeo. But no one seems to know anything, other than that he's facing surgery and probably many months of recovery."

"I know, and I feel bad about it. From what I've heard, he has thousands of loyal fans, but I'm sure Dr. Farha will do a news briefing later on today to bring everyone up to speed on his condition. Right now, there's not much to tell. And, by the way, he is not *my* Billy Bob."

Burgandi responded with a teasing huff. "You could have fooled me. He still hasn't told you why he wears that makeup?"

"No, but whatever the reason, I'm sure it's important to him."

"You don't think it's simply a gimmick?" Burgandi asked. "You know, something different and unusual to make him stand out from all the other bull riders and to keep people talking about him."

Dina considered her friend's words. "He's not like that. He's actually quite shy. You'd like him."

"He's sure got you wrapped around his little finger."

"Me? How can you say that? I feel sorry for him, that's all."

"Hey, this is your best friend you're talking to. I know you, Dina. I've seen you get interested in other guys, date them a few months, and then drop them for one reason or another. But I've never seen one sweep you off your feet like this man. And you haven't even seen his face!"

But I have seen his face! Dina wanted to scream out, but the loyalty she felt for him kept her from it.

Burgandi uttered a slight giggle. "What's he got that the others didn't have? Is there some secret magnetism you're not telling me about?"

"Of course not. He's just a very nice man. I like him."

Her friend huffed again. "A very nice cowboy/bull-riding man, and he's sure got you mesmerized."

"I am not mesmerized!" Dina replied indignantly. "As a nurse, I'm merely concerned about him, as I would be about any of my patients."

"You're forgetting one very important point. That man is *not* one of your patients. Plain and simple—you're there with him because you want to be."

"That's foolishness! Dr. Pratt asked me to accompany him to the hospital. Otherwise, I wouldn't have come."

"But once you were there, Dina, your responsibility was over. You had no more obligation to stay there than the EMTs or the man who drove the ambulance. Your job was finished."

Dina wanted to reply, to refute her words, but she couldn't. Ethically, Burgandi was right.

"Look, Dina, what you do with your life is your business but, as your best friend, I don't want to see you get hurt. I'm sure Billy Bob is as nice as you say he is, but I'm worried about what all this unusual allegiance you feel toward him will do to you. What if you fall for the guy?"

Dina gasped. "Fall for him? Are you crazy? He's everything I *don't* want in a man! I'd never fall for someone like him!"

"I hope you mean that."

"Just the idea of me falling for a *cowboy* is ridiculous, especially a bull-riding cowboy."

"What was it Shakespeare wrote in *Hamlet*? 'The lady doth protest too much, me thinks'? From my vantage point, it seems you're protesting way too much for someone whose sudden friendship with a near-stranger, who is a total opposite of the man she'd like to marry, becomes the primary focus of every breath she takes."

"Well, you're wrong," Dina told her adamantly. "Like I've already said, I feel sorry for him, that's all! End of discussion! Now, unless you have something else to chat about, this conversation is over."

"Other than to check on Billy Bob's condition and try to talk some sense into your head, I called to tell you that our committee is planning on finishing its work by late this afternoon, and we'll all be leaving for home in the morning. I was wondering if you'd be staying at the hospital or in our room tonight, because if you were staying at the hospital, I was going to offer to pack up your things."

"The committee is finishing today? I didn't think we'd be through until tomorrow afternoon."

"I didn't either, but things came together more easily than any of us had anticipated. By finishing today, that means everyone will have time to check out after breakfast, then head for home and arrive before dark." She paused. "You *are* planning on heading back to Omaha tomorrow, aren't you?"

six

Dina froze at her question. "I–I'm just surprised we're finishing so soon."

"Dina, be sensible. Forget about that man and go home like the rest of us. Surely you're not thinking of staying on."

"I—I don't know. I haven't decided."

"Look, sweetie, you're my friend. We've been best friends since our nurse's training days. And, knowing you and loving you like I do, I'll give you a bit of advice. After Billy Bob comes out of recovery and he is rational enough to know what you're saying, tell that cowboy good-bye, get in your car, head for Omaha, and never look back."

Dina knew her friend meant well, but Burgandi hadn't been around Will. He was more than just a cowboy. She hadn't been there when he'd shown more concern for the clowns who had tried to help him than he had for himself. She hadn't seen the respectful way he treated her, as well as the nurses and doctors who cared for him. No, the Will she'd come to know and respect in the few short hours she'd been around him was nothing like the man Burgandi thought he was. This man was kind and gentle and had a certain charm about him that was—

"Earth to Dina. Did you hear me? Are you heading back to Omaha or not?"

"Oh, Burgandi, I don't know," she said honestly. "It depends on what Dr. Farha says after he comes out of surgery, but I am staying with Billy Bob tonight. If his prognosis is good and he doesn't need me, I'll leave tomorrow."

"And if it isn't?"

"If it isn't—then I'll stay, at least through tomorrow afternoon. I can't leave him alone. You're a nurse. You know how difficult it is for our patients who have no one to be with them when they come out of surgery."

"Yes, I know, and I always feel bad for them, but that doesn't mean I'm obligated to stay by their side when my shift is over. I've said my piece, but it sounds like your mind is already made up."

"I'll slip away long enough in the morning to come back to the hotel. That way I can tell you and the others good-bye and pick up my things. Don't worry about packing for me. I really don't have that much."

"Promise you'll think about what I've said, Dina. I can't stand the idea of your being hurt. And considering how little you know about this man, and the fact that he *is* a bull rider, I'm afraid if you get involved with him, you'll have nothing but heartache."

"I'm not getting *involved* as you call it. I'm only helping someone who needs my help. Don't worry about me. I'll be fine." Dina hung up the phone then stood staring at the empty bed where a short time ago Will lay smiling at her. *I'll stay tonight and maybe tomorrow night if he needs me, then I'm gone.* But as she reached out and touched his pillow, she knew she was involved. To what extent, she couldn't be sure. All she knew was that leaving him and heading back to her busy life in Omaha was going to be one of the hardest things she had ever done.

Several others were already there when Dina made her way up to the surgical floor waiting room, apparently waiting for loved ones or friends who were also having surgery. She took a chair in a far corner then picked up a magazine and opened it.

A pretty, middle-aged woman leaned toward her. "You have someone in surgery?"

Dina nodded. "Yes, a close friend. How about you?"

"My husband. My sons and I were finally able to talk him into having his torn rotator cuff repaired. That thing has been paining him like you wouldn't believe."

"Have you heard the rumor?" the woman seated on her other side asked in a hushed voice. "Someone told us that Billy Bob—you know, the cowboy who got hurt at the rodeo the other night—is in this hospital."

Dina purposely raised her brows and tried to appear nonchalant. "Oh?"

"I've heard he's one of the nicest cowboys around but, for the life of me, I can't figure out why he'd wear that awful clown makeup. Do you suppose he's got some terrible scars on his face he doesn't want anyone to see?"

"Maybe he's just plain ugly!" the first woman said with a snort.

"Well, I know one thing," the second one replied. "I'm gonna keep my eyes open as I walk around the hospital halls. I've heard they're not giving out his room number, but I might just happen to get a peek at him."

"What makes you think you'd recognize him if you did see him? They probably took that stuff off his face when they brought him in here."

"Hey, not many men have as bushy a head of hair or a heavy beard like that cowboy does, and who wouldn't recognize those biceps of his? Believe me, I'll know him if I see him."

Good thing he let us cut his hair and trim up that beard, Dina thought.

"And if I do see him," the woman continued, waving her arm in an animated fashion, "I'm gonna run into his room and get his autograph. In fact, I might buy myself one of those disposable cameras and keep it in my purse. Wouldn't that be something if I could get a picture of that man without his makeup? I'll bet I could sell it to one of those rodeo magazines for big bucks."

"Yeah, but if he decided to sue you for invading his privacy, it might cost you a whole lot more than what you'd make."

Dina was glad when the doctor who'd performed the surgery on the first woman's husband came into the waiting room for his briefing. But hearing the women's discussion had made her begin to understand why Will had felt it necessary to keep his makeup on at all times. The thing she didn't understand was why he was so determined to keep his true identity a secret. What difference did it make?

Soon, both the doctor and the man's family left the room and she was alone again, her erratic thoughts her only companion.

As she had predicted, it was nearly two hours before Dr. Farha appeared. "We had quite a job putting Mr. Martin"—he paused and gave her a knowing wink—"back together." He glanced around and lowered his voice. "I was kind of surprised when I arrived at the hospital and learned Will Martin, the person I was going to be performing surgery on, was really Billy Bob. I didn't recognize him without that wild head of hair and that beard."

"We thought a trim was a good idea since we had to give the hospital his real name when we checked him in. You won't tell anyone who he is, will you?"

He shrugged. "Not unless it became absolutely necessary, which is highly unlikely. What he wants to be called elsewhere is his business."

"Thank you. I know Will would appreciate it."

Dr. Farha pulled a chair up in front of her and seated himself. "His shoulder was a mess and his arm wasn't much better. But with a few months of physical therapy, not to mention a lot of patience and hard work, he should regain full use of that arm."

"What about his leg?"

"I understand that bull pinned him against one of the steel posts as they came out of the chute. I haven't met a cowboy yet whose leg could take that kind of pressure without sustaining some type of injury. Not even rough-and-tumble cowboys like our Billy Bob. But it'll be okay. He's young and used to pain. He'll have to stay off of it for two or three days to give it time to heal. Sad thing is, with that shoulder, he won't be able to use crutches or a walker to support his weight. Which means he's going to be pretty much either bedfast or in a wheelchair until he can stand to walk on it." His face took on a smile. "He won't want to hop around on one leg, either."

"But he won't be able to ride bulls again, right?" she asked hopefully.

"He could, if he works hard at getting himself back in shape. That boy loves riding bulls!"

Her blood ran cold at the thought.

"But I'll be honest with you. He is going to have a lot of soreness. Most cowboys rebel when I tell them they are going to have to work with a physical therapist. They think they can do it on their own, but they can't. You're a nurse. You know what I'm talking about. If they don't do it right, they can cause even more damage." His expression brightened. "Dr. Grimes tells me you're a trauma nurse. I'm sure that means you've had some physical therapy training. Maybe you can help him."

"I'd like to, but he lives clear across the state from me."

He shrugged. "Too bad. Do you know of any physical therapists in his area you could recommend to him?"

She shook her head. None of what he was saying was good news. "No, and finding a good one may be difficult. The area where he lives is pretty isolated. The nearest hospital is probably a number of miles away."

Again he shrugged. "That definitely presents a problem. He

needs to get that therapy started as soon as he gets home."

"Do you have any idea when he might be released?"

He paused as if giving his answer some thought. "Barring any complications, I'd say in two days at the most."

"I know you're a busy man, Dr. Farha. I can't thank you enough for coming all the way from Denver."

"Like Dr. Grimes probably told you, I'm a big fan of rodeo and a part of the Justin Sportsmedicine Team. I'm like an old firehouse dog; that's why I bought my own plane. Tell me there's a rodeo anywhere nearby, or a cowboy who is hurt and needs my services, and I'm off and flying—literally." He rose and extended his hand. "Well, I've got to get back to Denver. Dr. Ken Flaming, the doctor who assisted me during surgery, is taking over for me now. Don't worry about your cowboy. This hospital has some fine doctors. While he's here, I'm sure he'll get the best of care. It's been nice meeting you, Miss Spark."

She started to tell him Will was *not* her cowboy, that they had only known each other a few days, but what difference did it make? She'd probably never see Dr. Farha again so she simply shook his hand, thanked him again, and said good-bye.

It seemed like forever before someone came to take her to Will's cubical in SICU. "He's still pretty groggy," the woman told her as Dina hovered over him. "Dr. Farha told us you were a trauma nurse. He left orders that we were to let you stay with him as long as you like. If he gets nauseated, just push the button and one of us will be here right away."

The nurse went about checking his vital signs, his IV, then the machines to which he was attached before nodding to Dina and leaving the two alone. Dina moved as close to the bed as she dared, then stood gazing at his nearly clean-shaven face. It wasn't that she hadn't liked his wild look; she had, though not at first. But that look had grown on her.

Somehow, it suited him, at least in his role as a bull rider. Maybe that wild hair had helped cushion his head when Gray Ghost had finally thrown him off his back and he had hit the ground. She straightened as a second nurse appeared in the doorway.

"Has he responded to you yet?"

She shook her head, then answered in a mere whisper, "No, but I've only been here a few minutes."

The nurse leaned over him and gave his good shoulder a slight shake. "Will, it's time to wake up. Your surgery is over and you have company."

He stirred slightly and seemed to be struggling to open his eyes.

She nodded toward Dina. "Go ahead. Talk to him."

After looping her hair over her ear, she again leaned close. "Will, it's me. Dina. Wake up, sleepyhead."

He responded with a slight moan.

"Dr. Farha said your surgery went just fine. With some physical therapy and a lot of work, you should be. . ." She paused. She wasn't about to say he should be riding bulls again. "You should be—like your old self."

"It might help if you'd take his hand and give it a good squeeze every once in a while. As I'm sure you know from experience, a personal touch does wonders for our patients."

She smiled as the woman headed for the door. "I will." Though his hand was rough and dry, she loved the feel of it as she cradled it in hers. It felt strong, earthy. He'd said he was a rancher. She could almost visualize him going about his daily chores—feeding cattle, mending fences, shoveling hay, cleaning stables. . . . Ranching was hard work. She knew, having grown up on a ranch herself. But, thanks to her father's injuries, her family's ranching days were a thing of the past. She had loved living on that ranch, helping care for the animals, riding her horse, watching the calves being born—but that was all behind her, never to be experienced again. She was a city gal now, living in one of Omaha's beautiful apartment complexes. She'd sold her horse and moved away the week her father had leased their Madison County ranch out to someone else. He and her mother had stayed in the house, but the ranching duties now fell upon other shoulders.

She startled as his fingers tightened around hers then relaxed. "Will, please wake up. I want to see those beautiful blue eyes."

He opened one eye, just the faintest crack, and stared at her, as if trying to focus on her image. "Dina?"

She bent nearer his face. "Yes, it's me. I'm here, just like I told you I would be."

"It's over?"

"Yes." With the tip of her finger, she pushed a wisp of hair away from his forehead. "All over. I'm right here."

"You're so bootiful. . . ."

She had to laugh. If people had any idea of the things that came out of their mouths when they were still under the effects of anesthetics, they would probably refuse to have surgery. One man she had attended in recovery had even confessed to stealing money from his employer.

When he began to gag, she burst into action and punched the button for the nurse. But rather than wait for her, she hurriedly began going through the cupboards in search of the nausea pan and, when she found it, lifted his head a bit and placed it beneath his chin. Although nausea was a perfectly normal reaction from someone just out of surgery, she felt sorry for him anyway and wished he didn't have to go through it. She could only imagine how uncomfortable being sick to his stomach was on top of everything else he was going through.

She stepped out of the way when the nurse entered and took over. Within minutes, his episode had run its course, the woman had cleaned his face with a wet cloth, and he was quiet again. Dina thanked her then moved back to his side and, once again, took his hand.

Though his eyes didn't open, the corners of his mouth lifted ever so slightly. "Glad you're here."

"I'm glad, too. I like being with you."

"Staying?"

"Yes, I'll be staying at the hospital all night. If they won't let me sleep here in the chair, I'll be in the waiting room just down the hall."

"Good." He sighed then took a several shallow breaths. "Sleepy."

"You go ahead and rest. I'll be close by if you need me."

"Pray?"

She smiled. "Yes, I'll keep praying for you."

❧

"There's a phone call for you at the desk," the nurse said in a whisper later that evening as her face appeared in the open doorway.

After a quick glance at Will, Dina hurried after her, then went in the direction the woman pointed and picked up the phone. "This is Dina Spark."

"Good, Dina, I was hoping you'd be there. I spoke with Dr. Farha. He gave me Billy Bob's floor number and said you were staying with him for a while." It was Dr. Pratt. "How's he doing? Did he come through the surgery okay?"

"Yes, he's getting along fine. The surgery went well. Dr. Farha said he should regain full use of his shoulder and arm if he works with a physical therapist like he should. He didn't seem overly concerned about his leg, just that it would take time to heal." Apparently, since Dr. Pratt had referred to Will as Billy Bob, Dr. Farha had kept Will's secret.

"That's good news. I'll pass the word around. I wanted to let you know they've gathered up Billy Bob's things, but the problem is no one is sure what to do with them. I removed his boots and spurs when they brought him into the Justin unit. If he's like most cowboys, he'll want to make sure he gets them back."

Dina searched her brain for an answer. She would like to tell them she had the key to Will's truck and would meet them there, so she could lock his belongings inside. But she wasn't sure, considering how far away Will had parked from the arena, that he wanted them to know which truck was his. All a resourceful person would have to do to learn his identity was get his truck's Nebraska license number and do a little detective work. "If someone is willing, they could deliver his things to the Nagle Warren Mansion. I'll be going back there early tomorrow morning to pick up my suitcase. I'll be glad to see that he gets them."

"Good. I'm sure that will work out fine. I'd bring them myself but I have a plane to catch. I'll put your name on the box and make sure someone takes it by. Other than his spurs and his boots, gloves, extra bull rope, that sort of thing, there wasn't much else, so everything should fit in one large box. Thanks, Dina. I know Billy Bob will appreciate your efforts. Be sure to tell him hello for me and wish him a speedy recovery. It was nice meeting you."

"I enjoyed meeting you, too, Dr. Pratt. I'll give him your message and I'll make sure he gets the box."

After she hung up, she stood gazing at the phone. *Exactly how am I going to do that? I'd planned to head out of town myself tomorrow. I can't just lug that heavy box into his hospital room and leave it. Most of the cowboys and others who are associated with rodeo will be gone by tomorrow, so none of them would be around—even if he trusted one of them to help him out. And how is he going to get back to Nebraska? He won't be able to negotiate crutches, and he certainly won't be in any condition to drive his old truck for weeks, maybe even months.*

A sudden realization hit her. *I'm the only one he has! There is no one else!*

Dina stayed by his side until about midnight then went to the hallway vending machine for a sandwich and something cold to drink. He was stirring when she reentered his room. "Hi, sleepyhead. I'm glad to see you're awake." She pulled the chair closer to his bed and smiled at him.

After blinking several times, he opened his eyes wide. "Is it over?"

"Yes, it's over. Dr. Farha said everything went well."

"Thanks for. . ."

"For being here? I told you I would." Inwardly she laughed. His question made her realize, since he hadn't been fully conscious when they'd had their last conversation, he wouldn't remember the part about telling her she was *bootiful*. Maybe this time, now that he was more fully awake, he'd remember things. "How do you feel? Are you in a lot of pain?"

"Not much."

"Are you sure there isn't someone you'd like me to call for you? An aunt or maybe a cousin who should know where you are?"

He shook his head. "No."

"Come on. Everyone has someone."

He merely shrugged his good shoulder. "Don't need someone. Just you."

"But my meetings here in Cheyenne are nearly over. I might be able to stay until noon tomorrow, but I have to get back to my job in Omaha."

His eyes widened. "Want you here."

"I have to go. My boss is expecting me to come back to work." She could tell her words upset him, but what else could she do? Like Burgandi had said, her obligation to him was over.

"You're my angel."

She bit at her emotions. "I'm no angel, Will. Just a nurse who happened to be on duty when you had your accident."

"No. *My* angel," he insisted.

Dina grinned. "You only think that because the anesthetics are still affecting you."

Smiling, the nurse flitted back into his room. "Well, I see our patient is finally awake and responding better now." She checked his vitals before taking hold of his foot through the sheet and giving it a squeeze. "By morning, we should be able to transfer you to a room on the post-op floor. If your wife's up to it, she can spend the rest of the night right there in that chair."

She kept her peace until the nurse left the room. "Great. She thinks I'm your wife."

He reached for her hand as he gave her sheepish grin. "Would that be so bad?"

She took it then entwined her fingers through his. "Of course not, but I should have told her."

"What difference does it make?"

She wanted to argue with him but what he'd said was true. Wife, sister, cousin? It really didn't make any difference what anyone thought. No one really cared who she was to him.

Though at times as they visited he still seemed a bit confused and unable to quickly sort out a few of his thoughts, they shared a fairly intelligent conversation before the other night nurse came in at about two o'clock to give him his pain medication and something to make him sleep.

She went about the task of straightening his covers and

filling his water glass then left them alone again. A few minutes later she returned, handing Dina a blanket and pillow. "You'll be needing these. Those recliners aren't nearly as comfortable to sleep in as they appear."

Dina took the items and thanked her. "I'm sure I'll be fine." She placed the things in the chair as soon as the woman left then gave her full attention to Will. "I wanted to let you know I'll be leaving for an hour or so in the morning. I have to go back to the hotel, pack up my things, and say good-bye to my friends, but I'll come back as soon as I can."

"I really like having you here. You promise you'll come back?"

"Yes, I promise. I like being here with you." She bent and lightly kissed his forehead. "It's after two. You'd better get to sleep. I'll be right there in that chair the rest of the night. If you need anything just tell me."

Other than Will moaning in his sleep a number of times, the rest of the night went fairly well. He stirred about five thirty when the night nurse came for her routine check, which gave Dina the opportunity to once again remind him she'd be going to the hotel, but she'd be back as soon as possible.

At seven thirty, she slipped quietly out of his room.

❧

Will slowly opened his eyes and gazed about the room, hoping to catch a glimpse of Dina, but she wasn't there. Ugghh, his mouth tasted like rotten eggs smelled, and his shoulder felt as if an elephant were sitting on it. He could shift his good leg but his injured leg refused to move. His entire body felt like he'd tangled with a bull and lost the fight—which he had. *Well, I didn't exactly lose*, he told himself with a trace of a smile. *Gray Ghost might have dragged me around the field, but I stayed on that awesome beast for the full eight seconds. Surely, that was a victory.*

But where was Dina? She'd promised she'd stay. He needed

her, not because of his helplessness, but because he couldn't get her off his mind.

"Well, good morning!"

He blinked then focused his eyes on the pleasant-looking woman coming through the door, carrying a tray. "What time is it?"

"A little past eight thirty. Are you hungry? I've brought breakfast." She placed the tray on the over-bed tray table then smiled at him. "Um, looks like your right arm isn't going to be of much help. I hope you're left-handed."

He shook his head. "No, I'm not."

"Well, don't worry about it. I can help you."

He didn't want *her* to help him; he wanted Dina.

He gazed at the tray. Not one thing on it looked good. As far as he was concerned they could take it away. "Yuk! That looks like the stuff my mom fed me when I was a baby. Can't I have some scrambled eggs, or at least a hard-boiled one?"

"Don't like what we've given you, huh? Well, I don't blame you. Our post-op menu is pretty boring, but it's what your body needs. You do want to get well, don't you?"

He nodded. "Yes, ma'am, but I'd sure rather have something else. I'm a meat-and-potatoes kind of guy."

"You men! You're all alike." She pushed the uninviting bowl of what looked to him like unbuttered, seasoned grits to one side then took the spoon and filled it with an equally disgusting-looking goldish-colored liquid from the other bowl. "Open up."

He did as told then sputtered as a weird flavor hit his tongue.

She gave him a sympathetic frown. "I know. It tastes awful, doesn't it?"

Again he nodded.

"But you have to eat. Come on, open up again. I may not

be as pretty as that wife of yours, but—"

"You've seen her?"

"Yes, not more than an hour ago. She said she had some errands to run and would be back as soon as she could. I imagine she'll be back in plenty of time to feed you your lunch but, in the meantime, you're going to have to put up with me."

He smiled at the congenial woman then opened his mouth. Dina hadn't left him. She was coming back. Though it was torture, he finished the bowl of chicken broth, or whatever it was, drank a full cup of coffee, and even consumed a small glass of juice. Once the helpful woman had adjusted his pillow and removed the tray, he settled back to await Dina's return.

Just the thought of seeing her lovely face made him smile. He'd never known anyone like her. He felt bad that she'd missed some of her meetings because of him, but how thankful he was that she had been on duty in the Justin trailer when they'd brought him in and then gracious enough to ride along with him in the ambulance. It had to be a *God thing*, he concluded, the way he was beginning to feel about her, that the two of them had been brought together.

He had to get that notion out of his head. Dina had simply been the one on duty when they'd carried him in on the gurney. She hadn't asked to ride to the hospital with him. That had been Dr. Pratt's idea. And what had he done? Gone all googly-eyed and begged her to stay with him, put the heavies on her by making her feel sorry for him, which probably did nothing but make her think of him as a wimp. Well, he wouldn't do that again. The best thing he could do for her was thank her for being there and send her back to Omaha. Though the last thing she would probably want was a relationship with cowboy who lived clear across the state, personally, he liked the idea. He had come to care for her in ways he never expected to care for a woman but he had to forget about her. Send her on her way, no matter how reluctant he was to see her go.

❧

By the time Dina reached the Nagle Warren Mansion, the rest of the committee members had already assembled around one of the tables and were enjoying their breakfast. She selected several items from the attractively displayed assortment on the cherrywood credenza then slid into the empty chair next to Burgandi, with a nod to everyone else. "Sorry I had to miss most of yesterday's meeting."

Celeste cocked her head to one side and eyed her. "So? How is your cowboy?"

Though Celeste's words, and the way she'd said them, agitated her, Dina responded with a friendly smile. "If you're asking about Billy Bob, he's doing as well as can be expected, considering the severity of his injuries."

Barbara leaned toward her. "It's nice that you've been staying with him, but you are going home today, aren't you?"

"She's not sure," Burgandi answered for her. "There's no one else to stay with him."

"Surely he has a relative, or at least a friend, who could stay with him."

Dina gave her head a shake. "No, there's no one, and he won't be able to drive himself home when they release him. I have no idea how he is going to get there."

Celeste appeared thoughtful. "Where does he live? Has he told you?"

"No, I only know it's a small town, miles away from a hospital."

Tracy did a *tsk-tsk*. "Too bad. From what the sports announcer on TV said about his injuries, he's going to need weeks, maybe months, of physical therapy. How's he going to do it if he lives that far from a hospital? If he doesn't have family to come and stay with him here, there probably isn't going to be anyone to take him to a physical therapist either."

Burgandi poked Dina's leg under the table then whispered, "Unless one would come to him."

Kitty's eyes widened. "I hope he has good insurance coverage. Working with a physical therapist every day, or even just several days a week, can get pretty expensive."

Dina took a final sip of juice then rose to her feet. "I'd like to stay but I have to—"

Burgandi rolled her eyes. "I know—get back to the hospital."

"No, I was about to say I have to pack up my things and put them in my car."

"By the way, someone from the hotel desk called our room last night. They're holding a box for you in the lobby."

Dina could tell by the look on her face that Burgandi was dying of curiosity, but she wasn't about to explain the box's contents or why it was delivered to her, so she feigned surprise. "Oh? I'll have to ask about it when I check out." She folded her napkin and placed it on the table. "I'm sorry to leave such good company but I really do have to get moving. It's been a delight seeing all of you again, and I'm looking forward to getting together with you at our convention." She placed a hand on Celeste's slim shoulder. "You've done a magnificent job on this, Celeste. Because of your close attention to detail, it seems everything came off without a hitch. I couldn't believe it when Burgandi told me the committee was finishing a day early. Even though I didn't do nearly as much work as the rest of you, I'm proud to have been a part of it." Before anyone had time to respond, she gave them a little wave and headed for the stairs.

She packed as quickly as she could, in hopes of getting out of the room before Burgandi finished her breakfast and came upstairs to confront her, but she didn't make it.

"You *are* staying, aren't you?" Burgandi asked, waving her arms as she flew into their room. "I knew it. I just knew it. You're in love with that guy. Dina, I thought you were smarter than that. I suppose next you're going to tell me it was love at first sight and you couldn't help yourself."

"I'm not in love with anyone, least of all a cowboy," Dina assured her indignantly.

"Yes, you are; it's written all over your face. How could you do it, Dina? A bull rider of all people? I've seen you turn down handsome, well-mannered, educated men with good jobs and brilliant futures ahead of them, guys who were crazy about you. Now you've gone gaga over some broken-down cowboy who wears silly polka-dot shirts and clown makeup! Sure he's popular, and probably making some pretty decent money at rodeos, but how long can that last? Especially considering his latest injuries? For all you know, the guy may have a wife and kids stashed away somewhere. He might even have a criminal record. Did you ever think that may be why he wants his face covered?"

"He's none of those things. He's a fine, decent man."

"You know that? After only two days, when much of that time he was still under the affects of drugs?"

"It's just something I know." She closed her suitcase lid with an impatient snap.

"Do you even know his real name?"

"Most of it."

"Where he lives?"

"Almost."

Burgandi threw her hands up in frustration. "Dina, how could you be in love with that man? Think! Don't be dazzled by his charm and the mystique that surrounds him. Go home. Go back to Omaha and forget him. Can't you see? He's using you! He knew when he came here he might get hurt. He's a big boy. Let him find someone else to take care of him. He is not—and I emphasize *not*—your responsibility. I'm sorry to be so emotional about this, but I'm your friend. I can't stand idly by and watch you get hurt."

Dina wrapped her arms about her friend. "I told him I would stay today but I was going home tomorrow, and that's what I intend to do. Does that make you feel any better?"

"Yes, if you actually mean it and are not just saying it to get me off your case."

"I do mean it."

Burgandi sighed. "I should have known you were too smart to do something that foolish. Can you forgive me for my raving and ranting?"

Dina tightened her grip. "I already have."

❧

Since she wasn't quite sure what to do with the box when she got to the hospital, she temporarily left it locked in her trunk. Will was waiting for her with the head of his bed raised, cradled in clean sheets, fresh from a sponge bath, his hair still damp. "Well, don't you look nice?" she asked as she breezed into his room.

"Thanks." His warm smile made her smile. "I was hoping you'd come back."

She pulled her purse strap from her shoulder then placed her purse in the chair before moving up close to his bed. "If you knew me better, you'd know I always keep my promises."

His smile broadened. "I'd like to know you better."

"And I'd like to know you better. You know I'm Dina Spark, a trauma nurse who lives in Omaha. All I know about you is that your real name is William Martin, and you're a rancher/bull rider who lives somewhere in southwestern Nebraska. That's about it."

"I'd tell you more, if I could."

"When I visited with my friend at the hotel this morning, she said the best thing I could do would be to head back to Omaha and forget about you, that I didn't know the real you—only what you wanted me to believe, which may not be the truth. Truth is very important to me."

He winced at her words. "She's probably right, but you're not going to take her advice, are you?"

"I told you I'd stay until tomorrow, and I will, but I'll need to leave no later than noon. I need to get back to my own life. I like you, Will, I really do, and I've enjoyed every minute of being with you, but your recovery is not my responsibility. Surely when you got into bull riding you knew something like this was bound to happen eventually. Didn't you have a plan in mind? Someone you could call in case of an emergency like this?"

He shook his head as he lowered his gaze. "Not really. I never expected something like this to happen. I'm very grateful for all you've done. I realize that, like the others who brought me here in that ambulance, you could have walked off, left me, gone back to whatever you were doing, and thought of me as nothing more than another patient among the many you see every day. But you didn't. You stayed."

"BUT—"

"Let me finish. I wish there was some way I *could* repay you for staying but"—he gestured his good hand toward his injured shoulder then his leg—"until these things heal and I'm back on my feet, there is no way I can do it. Maybe I can send you a present. Just know you are the best thing that has ever happened to me."

"No presents, please. I'd do more if I could, but I can't. I have to get home."

He gazed at her, his blue eyes seeming to penetrate her

very soul. "You're a pretty little thing. Did anyone ever tell you how beautiful you are?"

She sent him a shy smile. "Yes, you. You did."

His brows rose. "I did? When? I've wanted to tell you but I don't remember actually doing it."

"The afternoon you came out of surgery." Her smile turned to an embarrassed grin. "You probably don't remember it because you were still a bit loopy at the time."

"Good for my subconscious mind. It did what I'd wanted to do a number of times, because you are beautiful."

Though Dina often received compliments from her friends and coworkers, she never knew how to respond. "Thank you. It's nice of you to say so."

"I only said it because you are. You're a real knockout, Dina. I envy the guy who marries you."

She felt a flush rise to her cheeks. "I–I'm not sure that marriage thing will happen too soon. Not unless Mr. Right comes along. My standards are pretty high."

"Yeah, I hear that. You sure wouldn't want to make a mistake. As Christians, I'm sure we both think marriage should be forever."

"Oh, yes, for sure. Being married to the wrong person could be miserable."

The silence in the room was palpable.

Finally, lifting his head, Will motioned toward the door. "I've been thinking, as much as I hate to see you go, if you leave now you can still get to Omaha before dark. Go on, Dina. Don't worry about me. Dr. Flaming and the nurses are giving me great care. I'm sure you need to get back to your life."

"But I promised I'd stay until tomorrow."

"I know you did but, believe me, other than the fact that I enjoy your company and your smiling words of encouragement, there really isn't any reason for you to stay. Go on home. The doctor said they'd be releasing me in a day or two, so I'll be going home, too." With that, he turned his head to one side and closed his eyes. "I'm getting kind of sleepy. If you don't mind, I'd like to take a nap."

"Are you sure? I could stay."

With his eyes still closed, he took a deep breath and let it out slowly. "No. Go on back to Omaha. Like I said, I'll be fine."

"But I have your boots and spurs."

He opened his eyes and stared at her. "How did *you* get them? I figured they were long gone and I'd never see them again."

"Dr. Pratt had someone deliver them to my hotel, along with a few other items you'd left behind. I have them locked in the trunk of my car."

He continued to stare at her, as if trying to come up with a place she could leave them.

"The box isn't heavy; it's bulky, but I think it will fit in your closet. Do you want me to bring it up here?"

"I hate to ask you to, but I sure don't want to lose my boots, and especially not my spurs. They're kind of special to me."

"You didn't ask. I volunteered. I'll do it now." She glanced down at the sheet covering his leg. "By the way, how are you going to get home when they release you? Even though you have one hand to steer, with your injured leg being your right one, you won't be able to drive yourself."

He shrugged. "I can probably find someone to drive me."

"But all the rodeo people you know have gone home."

"Then I'll hire someone."

"They had to cut your shirt and pant leg to get to your wounds. You don't even have clothes to wear."

"I can call one of the local stores and have jeans, a shirt, underwear, and socks delivered. That's all I need."

He seemed to have an answer for everything.

"Then I'll be back in a little while." With an assortment of confused feelings, she turned and walked out into the hall.

❧

Will stared at the ceiling. When he had promised himself he would send Dina on her way, he'd had no idea it would be so hard. The idea of never seeing her again made him ache. He wished there could be something between them but she was on her way up in her profession. He might still have a few good years in him, if he were ever able to ride bulls again but, after that, he'd be on his way down. A man's body could only take so much abuse. He'd already had his share. When his bull-riding days were over, he would go back to being nothing more than a plain old cowboy.

He closed his eyes and listened to the slight sound of her heels clicking across the marble floor as she crossed the room and opened the closet, then the sound of the box as she scooted it into the closet. He held his breath as her footsteps came closer to the bed and she opened and closed the drawer of his nightstand. When all sound ceased, he visualized her blue eyes gazing down at him. Every bone in his body cried out for him to take her in his good arm, kiss her, and tell her how much he cared for her. But what right did he have to do such a foolish thing? Besides, she would probably be furious with him for being so brash and they would end up parting on bad terms.

What is she doing? Simply standing there looking down at me? He tried to keep his breathing even, but with the emotions raging inside him at the thought of letting her walk out of his life it was impossible.

How much longer could he lie there without giving himself away? She'd brought his boots and spurs. Why didn't she leave? He was about to open his eyes when he felt her warm breath on his face, then the sweet touch of her lips as they grazed his cheek. He lay as still as stone, his heart hammering against the wall of his chest. When he felt her lips touch his cheek, he thought he would die from gladness. He'd never felt anything so delicious. It was all he could do to keep from kissing her back. How he wished he hadn't faked sleep. But if he hadn't, maybe she would have put the box in the closet, said a simple good-bye, and left without kissing him.

"Wake up, Will," she murmured softly, her lips feathering against his.

He opened his eyes slowly. She was so close he could see the soft green flecks in her blue eyes. "You're back," he said, trying to sound as though he had just awakened from a sound sleep.

She moved a fraction away from him. "The box containing your boots, spurs, and those other things is in the closet. I hope you didn't mind my waking you but I couldn't leave without saying a proper good-bye."

"Thanks for bringing the box. A cowboy isn't a cowboy without his spurs." Oh, how he wanted to reach up and kiss her.

"Well, I guess I'd better be going. I really want to make it to Omaha before dark."

He nodded. "Yeah, good idea. Have a safe trip."

"You will look me up if you ever get to Omaha, won't you?"

"I've only been there once. It's not likely I'll get there again, but you never know." He sucked in a deep breath and held it when her finger touched his cheek.

"Then I guess this is good-bye. It's been nice knowing you, Will."

"It's been nice knowing you, too, Dina. And thanks again."

Before he knew what was happening, she bent and kissed him on the lips again, this time, long and lingering. Then, before he could respond or say another word, without even a backward glance in his direction, she was gone.

His hand slowly rose and touched his lips.

Dina may be walking out of his life, but he'd remember her beautiful face and that kiss forever.

seven

"Whoa, Miss Spark, wait up!"

Dina turned at the sound of her name. "Oh, hi, Dr. Flaming."

"I thought you would like to know, since Mr. Martin is doing so well, I plan to release him tomorrow."

"Tomorrow? I hadn't realized it would be that soon."

"Well, there's really nothing more we can do for him here. The rest of his recovery is up to him."

She asked a few questions about the type of therapy he thought would be best and then, once again, thanked him for his part in Will's recovery.

"No thanks needed." He glanced at his watch. "Oops, I'm late. I have to be going, too. Have a safe drive back to Omaha."

Dina sat in her car a full ten minutes before inserting the key in the ignition and giving it a turn. The news that they were going to release Will that soon had come as a real shock. "I don't care if he is leaving early and has nothing to wear and no one to drive him, it's not my problem," she told herself aloud, thumping her hands on the steering wheel in frustration. "Let him find his own way home. He's nothing but an arrogant—self-centered—independent—broken-down—bull rider! How dare Burgandi accuse me of being in love with someone like him! A man who wears makeup and silly shirts—and—and rides bulls?"

She yanked the gearshift into reverse, hurriedly looked both ways, backed, then fell in line with the other cars waiting to exit the hospital's parking lot. *Okay, I admit I felt sorry for him.*

And was maybe a little dazzled by the mystique that surrounds him, but I could never love him.

As the cars ahead of her began to move, she inched cautiously forward. *If I were interested in finding a man, which I'm not at this stage of my life, a rodeo would be the last place I'd look for him.*

When she came to the intersection of Warren and 24th, though she was tempted to turn right and circle back to the hospital and Will, she made a left at 24th, then turned south onto Central and headed toward I-80 and home. *That man is on his own now. There is nothing else I can do for him. But pray,* she reminded herself as the miles ticked by on her odometer. *In a few days he'll be nothing but a memory.* But in her heart she knew forgetting him wasn't going to be that easy, not after the once-in-a-lifetime experience the two had shared together.

Nearly an hour later, when she reached I-80's exit 21 near Kimball, Nebraska, she changed her mind, pulled off the road, and dialed a familiar number on her phone.

Her boss answered on the first ring.

Next, she called her mother. "Hi, Mom. I know you're going to think I'm crazy but I won't be back to Omaha for another week or two. A friend of mine has been injured and needs a ride home and someone to stay a few days to help with physical therapy."

"Oh, sweetheart, I'm sorry to hear about your friend's injuries. Is it anyone I know?"

Dina hesitated, not wanting to upset her mother by letting her know the person was not only a man but one she barely knew. "No, it's someone I met in Cheyenne. I've already called my boss. She okayed my using my vacation time."

"Was this another nurse?"

Not wanting to lie to her mother, she decided to give her

the whole truth. "No, a bull rider. It's a long story. I met him at the rodeo—"

"What were you doing at a rodeo? You hate bull riding!"

"Yeah, I know. I wasn't there to attend the rodeo. I was helping out in the Justin Sportsmedicine trailer and ended up riding to the hospital in the ambulance with him. He lives not far from Burgandi, and since I was driving home in his direction, I offered to drive him."

"And you're staying there? At the man's house? That's not like you, Dina."

"He and his mom live on the family ranch in Belmar, a little town in southwest Nebraska. Don't worry, he's not much of a threat. He isn't able to get around on his own. I'm only staying until he can find a physical therapist to take my place." She went on to explain both his injuries and his prognosis. "He needs my help, Mom. It's the right thing to do."

"Call me every day. I want to know you're getting along okay. Don't take any chances. If he gets—well, you know—get out of there fast."

Dina laughed. "He's not that kind of man, Mom, and even if he was, with his injuries he'd have a hard time catching me." They visited a few more minutes then she hung up, still smiling as she thought of Will chasing her with his bad leg and an unusable arm.

❧

Will did everything he could to keep his mind off Dina, but nothing worked. Her lovely vision was always with him. He couldn't even nap without dreaming about her.

"Good morning. How's my star patient?"

He turned his head at the sound of his doctor's voice. "Good morning, Dr. Flaming. I'm doin' okay."

Dr. Flaming glanced at his chart then moved to the side of the bed. "Actually, you're doing better than okay. Fortunately, much of what Dr. Farha and I had to do to your knee we were able to do using arthroscopic surgery, which is helping shorten your recovery time. In fact, by tomorrow, you'll be ready to go home. I'm sure that's good news."

He gave his good shoulder a slight shrug. "Yeah, I guess it is."

The doctor frowned. "Is there a problem?"

"No, not really. Since I won't be able to drive myself, I'm just not sure how I'll get there."

"I would think, as popular as you are, there would plenty of people who would be willing to drive you."

"Yeah, probably. I'll think of something."

"Then I'll see you in the morning." He headed for the door. "I'll sign your release and you can go home."

"Thanks, Dr. Flaming. I appreciate all you've done for me." As the doctor left his room, Will leaned his head against the pillow and closed his eyes. He knew he had no right to ask God why this catastrophe had happened to him. He had put himself in harm's way. No one had twisted his arm and made him do it. He'd known from the moment he'd straddled himself over that bull's back he was inviting injury. He'd made the decision; now it was up to him to suffer the calculable consequences. What did they call it? Paying the piper? He'd danced to Gray Ghost's tune; now it was his turn to pay the piper, whatever the costs. *Lord, You know the mess I've gotten myself into. I really need Your help. Getting this battered body back to Belmar is going to take nothing short of a miracle.*

❧

Dina couldn't keep from smiling as she strode across the hospital lot nearly four hours later, a shopping bag in her hand. Her unexpected decision had been the right one. She could feel it in her bones. James 4:17, one of the scriptures she had learned as a child, kept ringing through her mind. *"Therefore to him that knoweth to do good, and doeth it not, to him it is sin."* What she was about to do was good, the right thing to do. Surely God would be pleased.

She smiled a friendly hello to several nurses as she exited the elevator and swung left. The beat of her heart seemed to quicken as she turned and entered a very familiar room.

"Dina? What are you doing here? I thought you went back to Omaha."

Grinning with anticipation and excited to see how Will would react when she explained, she moved close to the bed and placed her hand on his good shoulder. "I've come to drive you home!"

"You can't. You're supposed to get back to your job."

"I had some vacation time coming so I called my boss, explained your circumstances, and asked if it would be okay if I used it. She said yes, she could find someone to take my place, and here I am!" Out of habit, she began tugging at the covers on his bed, straightening them for him as she had done since he'd been admitted.

"But—"

She put her finger to his lips to silence him. "I know what you're going to say. That I shouldn't use my vacation time that way, and if I drive you home in my car your pickup will be left in Cheyenne with no way for you to get it." She paused long enough to grab a breath. "My friend Burgandi and her parents live less than fifty miles from where we met. They'll drive to Cheyenne this weekend, get your pickup, and drive it back to their house—if that's okay with you. They would never tell anyone who you are, Will. Then, when you feel like it, you can have someone drive you those few miles to their place to pick it up, and no one will know where you live and you can remain as mysterious as ever, whatever your reason for wanting to do so. See, it's all taken care of. You don't have to worry about a thing. From what you've said, I assume you live with your mother. If it's all right with her, I'll stay at your place for a few days, help you with your physical therapy until we can get someone else lined up, then I'll go back to my life in Omaha. You came to my rescue, now it's my time to come to yours."

"My mom would be happy to have you there, but—"

"Okay then, don't try to argue with me. I'm driving you."

"But—"

"I know. You don't have any clothes to wear home." Spinning around, she took the shopping bag from the chair where she'd left it and dumped its contents onto the bed in front of him. "See? All taken care of. New shirt, jeans, underwear, and socks. I even got you a new pair of sports shoes. I checked the size on your boots, so I know they'll fit."

"But you've already done. . ."

She reached out and took hold of the hand that had become so familiar to her. Despite its roughness, she adored the feel of his skin against hers. "Quit making such a big deal out of it. It wasn't as if I really did anything. Mostly, I just stayed here with you."

His smile broadened into a grin. "Having you here is what has kept me going."

"Then it's settled. I'm driving you home."

The physical therapist came in about two o'clock and spoke with them, explaining the type of exercises that would be necessary to bring his body back to where it had been before his accident and how often he should do them.

"I'm really glad you'll be helping him," she told Dina after handing her some written information she thought would be helpful. "Hopefully by the time you have to leave him, he will have found a good therapist to take your place."

They both thanked her then spent the rest of the afternoon

and most of the evening either visiting or watching television. When the ten o'clock news program ended, she switched off the TV, pulled the blanket up over him, then curled up in the recliner.

By the time Dr. Flaming came in early the next morning, Will had not only finished his breakfast, he was dressed, ready, and eager to leave.

❧

Dina settled herself in the driver's seat then turned to gaze at the tired face of the man sitting next to her. Even with the assistance of the two men from the hospital, it had taken some doing to get him out of the wheelchair and into the front seat of her small car. But, with the help of the pillows she'd bought—one to prop behind his shoulder and one to put under his leg—Will finally found a position that was comfortable and began to relax.

She shoved the key into the ignition and smiled at her passenger. "Ready?"

He nodded. "Yeah, but now I'm really worried."

"About what?"

"I'm wondering how I'm going to get from your car into the house when I get home. Those two big, strong orderlies aren't going to be there to help me, and I'm way too big for you and my mom to carry."

As she pulled out of the parking lot, she sent him a playful grin. "We could rent a forklift."

"That's funny, but this isn't a joke. It's serious. With my bad leg, I can't even crawl."

She felt sorry for making light of his situation. "What would you say if I told you I rented a wheelchair? It's in the trunk."

His expression brightened. "Did you, really?"

"Hey, I'm a nurse. I think about those things. It'll probably still be a struggle to get you into it, but we'll make it. Don't worry about it. You're dealing with a professional."

"I should have known. You think of everything."

"Not everything, but I try. It's about two-and-a-half hours to Ogallala. I thought we'd stop there for lunch." She gave him an impish smile. "Are you ready to tell me your full name or am I going to have to read it off your mailbox when we get to your ranch?"

He grinned back. "I guess, after you've been so patient with me, it's only right that I tell you. It's William *Robert* Martin."

She threw her head back with a laugh. "Oh, I get it! William Robert Martin—Billy Bob!"

"Yep, that's me. Now you know."

"Now I feel like I'm privy to some big national secret."

"Hardly, but the name has served me well."

"But why use it? Why not just go by your real name? And why the makeup? Was it, like some people say, all just some big promotional idea? To get you noticed by the fans?"

He huffed. "I wish I could say that's why I did it but, no, promotion had nothing to do with it."

She frowned. "Then why? I don't understand."

He gazed at her for a moment, as if considering his answer before voicing it. "I'm going to tell you, Dina, but not here. About fifty miles after we leave I-80, we'll be driving past the little town of Hayes Center. Turn off there, find a nice shady tree, and park, and I'll tell you my whole sordid story."

"Why there? That's a long way from here. Why not tell me now?"

"Number one. Because I'm sleepy." He stifled a yawn then leaned his head against the headrest and closed his eyes.

"And number two?"

He opened one eye and peered at her. "Because I don't want to tell you while we're driving down the road at seventy miles an hour. I want to tell you face-to-face. It's better that we wait until we get to Hayes Center."

She wanted to argue with him but decided not to. He'd agreed to tell her: that was something. She'd just have to wait. By the time they reached I-80, he was sound asleep.

After a pleasant lunch at Ogallala, she continued on to Highway 83, turning south toward Wallace where it intersected with Highway 25. "You'll have to guide me from here," she told him, after glancing in her rearview mirror. "I've never been this way before."

"We've got another fifty miles to go on this road before we hit Hayes Center. It's sure nice to be back in Nebraska again. I love this state." He shifted his weight then let out a slight groan.

"I wish my car was bigger. I hate it that you're so cramped up. Too bad you can't get out and stretch your legs."

"That would be nice, but we both know that won't work. I'm fine. Don't worry about me."

Her anticipation rose with each mile as they headed toward Hayes Center. It seemed to take forever before the city's road sign appeared in the distance.

"The town is to your left, a mile or so off this road," he told her, pointing east.

She made the turn then drove through the tiny town until they came to a tall tree, its branches fanning out over the dirt street, its thick green leaves filtering out the hot afternoon sun. "This okay?"

When he nodded she parked and turned off the engine then rolled down her window and twisted in the seat to face him. "I'm listening."

eight

Instead of responding, Will just sat there, staring straight ahead, wondering where he should begin. How much he should tell her. . .

"Are you okay?"

"Yeah, I'm okay."

She reached to help him adjust the pillows when he tried to angle his body more toward hers. "You have to be tired. We can go on if you want—you can tell me your story later."

He was tired, and he'd like nothing more than to head on to Belmar, lie down in his own bed, and stretch out his limbs. Sitting cramped up in her small car had been much harder on him than he'd let on. "No. I'd rather tell you now."

She gazed at him for a moment, her eyes betraying her concern for him. "You sure you feel up to it?"

No, I hurt like crazy but, right now, that isn't important. What is important is being honest with you. "Just let me talk, okay? You have to know everything before we get to the ranch."

A frown creased her brow. "Why before then?"

"Because, Dina, you'll be the first one to hear my story. No one else knows it. Not even my mom."

Her eyes rounded. "Your own mother doesn't know?"

"No, but I hope after you hear me out you'll understand why I haven't told her. Just sit back and listen, okay?"

She nodded.

"Several years after my parents married, my mother's father died and she inherited our ranch. Unfortunately, she also inherited the huge mortgage he'd put on it, as well as a number of bills he'd left unpaid. Mom loved the ranch. My dad hated it, which meant my mom ended up being the one who ran it and did most of the chores. Until us four kids came along." He paused with a half smile. "Actually, about the only thing he was good at was giving my mom babies."

When he turned to look at Dina, she was smiling, too.

"Anyway, he was always after my mom to sell the ranch, which she refused to do, knowing that by the time the mortgage and the bills were paid off they'd be walking away with nothing. To her, that ranch meant security. As long as she could scrape up enough to keep the bank happy, we had a roof over our heads, meat on the table from the cattle we could raise, and vegetables from our garden."

Dina gave her head a sad shake. "Poor woman. Sounds like she had it pretty rough."

"She did, but she rarely complained and never thought of us as poor. Lacking in some of the nicer things of life, yes, but never poor."

"I didn't mean—"

Will lifted his hand. "I know. We might not have had as much as our neighbors, but we were rich in other ways. No one ever had a better mother. She raised us kids to be strong in body and mind, and strong in the Lord. For that, I'll always be thankful. Our faith is what got us through when everything else failed. By the time I was ten years old, I had taken over a good part of my mom's responsibilities and I was literally running the ranch, under her watchful eye, of course, and I did a good job. Summers, I even helped some of the other ranchers in order to earn extra pay to put in the sugar bowl where my mom kept the next month's mortgage payment. My dad? We didn't see much of him. He never did anything around the ranch, but he did work an odd job now and then, digging ditches, whatever he could find, but most of his time was spent at the pool halls or playing horseshoes for money. He turned into quite a gambler. Well, to make this very long story short, he came to me the morning of my twelfth birthday and told me—because my mom was pregnant and about ready to go into labor—he was going to drive into McCook to buy me a present and, when he came back, we'd all have cake and ice cream and celebrate."

"I'll bet that made you happy."

Will smiled. "Yeah, it did. He'd never bought me a present before. I waited for him all day. . . ." He felt the smile fade as he took on a frown. "But he didn't come back."

Dina flinched at his words. "Ouch, that must have hurt. Did he apologize?"

"No. In fact, we never saw him again."

"Ever? He just up and left?"

"That's exactly what he did. To make matters worse, the next morning my mom discovered he'd taken every penny out of the sugar bowl. Then, when she went to the bank to tell them she'd be late with her payment, she found out he had also taken the few dollars in savings she'd accumulated toward buying another calf to raise for our herd. Plus, he owed others in town, and soon they were constantly at our door, trying to collect those debts from my mom."

"How could he do such a thing? To his own family? Especially when his wife was about to go into labor?"

"Beats me. He walked off and left the woman he had vowed to care for and protect, after giving her four kids and leaving her buried in debt, and never looked back. And I've hated him for it ever since. What he did was unforgivable."

"I know."

He drew back in surprise. "What? No lectures on how a Christian should be willing to forgive? No comments on how my dad is as much a child of God as you and me?"

"No, I can't point a finger at you without pointing one at myself."

"Dina, what do you mean? Point one at yourself?"

"I'll tell you later, I promise. Right now, I want to hear about you."

"Okay, but I'm going to hold you to it." He uttered a slight moan as he shifted his leg. "Well, like I said, I was running the ranch by then. My two younger brothers helped as much as they could—my sister, too—but I was the one who ran things, with my mom overseeing everything, of course. I knew from going over the books with her that if we didn't do something, we weren't going to be able to keep that mortgage paid. I'd had a love of bull riding ever since I was old enough to straddle the old barrel another kid and I suspended between the trunks of four trees. Every spare moment I could get, I'd ride that old barrel and got pretty good at it. So, when one of our neighbors offered to let me try to ride his bull, I took him up on it. I was sixteen by then. Next thing I knew, I was ready for our local rodeo."

"So that's how you got into bull riding!"

"Yeah, at first my mom didn't mind, but then one of the guys, who shouldn't have been riding bulls in the first place, got a little cocky and stayed on the field too long after he'd been thrown off, shaking his fist in the bull's face, challenging him to come after him. Then when the bull did, he tripped over his own feet and fell."

Dina's hand flew to cover her mouth as she gasped. "Oh, no! What happened?"

"The bull trampled him to death, right there in front of our eyes. My mom was so scared she went crazy. She told me right then and there—absolutely no more bull riding for me. It scared me bad, too, but it also taught me a lesson. To never take my eye off a bull and to get off that field as quick as possible and let the clowns handle him. But, even though I knew I was riding without my mom's knowledge, I couldn't stop. I was twenty by that time and, as a grown man I felt it was up to me to make my own decisions and I told her so. I had just begun to make a little money—money we badly needed. So, since she was used to me spending time away from home by hiring myself out to other ranchers, she didn't suspect a thing when I kept taking off on weekends to do rodeo. I'd just tell her I had work to do out of town."

"That's when you started wearing the mask?"

He shook his head. "No, I just made sure any rodeos I entered were far enough from home my mother wouldn't hear about it. Anyway, when I was twenty-four, and riding even better, and word about the high scores I was making began to get around, I decided I'd better either quit or figure out a way to ride so my mom wouldn't accidentally find out. I couldn't quit. Those winnings were beginning to mount up, enabling me to pay the mortgage payment each month and actually put a little money in the bank. About that same time, while watching some of the cowboy clown bull fighters on TV, I came up with the idea of wearing a painted-on half-mask and the funny shirts, letting my hair and beard grow longer, adding a few extra pounds, and changing my name. So over that winter, I took about four months off to let it grow and add the pounds. I sure didn't want to register under my own name so, overnight, I became Billy Bob, the bull rider who came out of the blue, one that no one knew or recognized."

Dina let out a sigh and gave her head a shake. "And your mom never knew. That's why you didn't want me to call her and let her know about your injuries."

"Yes."

"But you said you'd had other injuries. Didn't she wonder about those?"

"Naw, I'd tell her they were all in a day's work, which was true."

She leaned back in the seat and stared straight ahead. "And you did all of this to save your family's ranch."

"Yes, and take care of a lot of other family expenses. Remember, I had three siblings to help care for. My two brothers, who never cared about staying on the ranch, are out on their own now. Ben is working in West Virginia and Jason is in college, studying for his Masters. My little sister Teresa, the one Mom was carrying when my dad left, is in college, too."

Dina took hold of his good hand and smiled up at him sympathetically. "And now you're on your way home and you're going to have to tell her."

He hung his head. "Yep, and I'm not looking forward to it. It's going to be one of the hardest things I've ever done."

"That's why you wanted to tell me before we got there."

He nodded. "Yes. Telling you was almost as hard as it's going to be to tell her, but I had to do it. Does it make any sense to you, when I say I'm both ashamed of what I've done, yet proud that I did it? Because I am proud. Rodeoing made it possible for me to nearly pay off the mortgage on our ranch. Since I've been handling the books and writing the checks, although my mom doesn't even know it yet, my plans are to have it paid off in one year, by her fifty-ninth birthday, and throw a big burning-of-the-mortgage party for her. That way, my sweet mama, who was born on that place, the place where she bore and raised her children, will also be able to die there."

❧

Dina dabbed at her eyes with her free hand, so touched by his words she could barely speak. "I had no idea."

"Don't you see, Dina? What I've done, I didn't do for me. I did it for my mom and for our family. While I admit I love the thrill of riding bulls and the roar of the crowd when

I've had a good ride, participating in rodeos was my means to an end. A job that paid me far better than any other job I could find in our area, one I could do while also taking care of the ranch. Why do you think I drive that old truck? Because every penny I've made has gone into that ranch, its improvement, or our savings, so my mom wouldn't lose it."

"And that's why you're going to *keep* riding bulls."

"Yeah. With the herds and the bulls we have now, in a little over a year, with the ranch paid off, our cattle operation should be self-sustaining and provide a fairly decent living."

"*Then* you'll quit the rodeo business?" Oh, how she hoped his answer would be yes.

A shy grin formed beneath his mustache. "Someday maybe, but not that soon. I plan to ride for as long as I'm able and then go into business for myself. I'll still be around rodeos. I just won't be riding the bulls myself. I'm hoping to eventually raise several mean, cantankerous bulls as rodeo stock for others to ride." He chuckled. "Billy Bob's Bulls. Don't you think that has a nice ring? Hopefully, my reputation as a winning bull rider will open a few doors for me."

He's going to keep riding bulls? His words really upset her. Why hadn't the man learned his lesson? Well, it was his life, not hers. What he wanted to do with it was his business.

"Well, that's pretty much it. Do you hate me for it?"

"Hate you? I could never hate you—especially not after what you just told me about riding because of your family's ranch. Your motives were pure. If I would have been in your shoes—I probably would have done the same thing." She gave him a half smile. "Well, maybe not ride bulls, though at one time I had aspirations to rise to the top in barrel racing. But I would have done whatever was necessary to care for my mom." Her heart skipped a beat when he allowed his thumb to rove over the back of her hand.

His brows rose. "Barrel racing! You never told me."

"I know. I should have told you but after all the fuss I've made about you and bull riding, I guess I hated to admit that I, too, had been caught up in the thrill of participating in rodeo."

"When did—"

"We'll talk about my barrel racing days later, but right now we need to get you home." Reluctantly, she pulled her hand free from his and reached for the key in the ignition, giving it a turn.

They rode the rest of the way in silence as Dina ran his story over and over in her mind. She could only imagine how hard it was for him to tell her all those things. No wonder he had worked so hard at keeping his identity a secret. It was all for his mother.

nine

"Turn left at that next road," he told her just before they reached the little town of Belmar. Two miles later, when they came to a mailbox marked MARTIN, she swung a right and headed down the dusty road toward the old farmhouse that loomed in the distance, pulling up in front of the porch when they reached it.

"It's beautiful!" she said, meaning it. She gazed appreciatively at the two-story frame house, with its brown shutters, flower-filled window boxes, and fretwork-trimmed porch. "No wonder you and your mother wanted to keep this place in the family."

Before he could comment, the front door opened and a feisty little woman donned in an apron came flying out and rushed down the stairs toward them. "Her friend has a car similar to yours," he explained, dipping his head low. "She thinks it's her. She's really gonna be upset when she finds out it's me."

The woman's smile disappeared when she reached Dina's side of the car. "Oh, sorry. I thought you were someone else. What can I do for you?"

Dina gestured in Will's direction. "Someone here wants to see you."

The woman bent, giving her a full view of the front seat, let out a cry of joy when she realized it was her son, then raced around to the other side and flung open the door.

❧

Will held his breath as she moved toward him, knowing no matter how glad she was to see him he was in for the worst verbal thrashing he'd ever had. As she flung his door open, despite the pain vibrating through his shoulder and arm, he swiveled in the seat to face her. "Hi, Mom."

Instead of ranting at him, like he'd expected, she threw her arms around his neck and began to cry, calling out between sobs, "You're home! I've been so worried. You're home. Praise the Lord for answered prayer." Then backing off a bit, she surveyed the shirt he was wearing, noting how only his left arm was in a sleeve with the other sleeve merely draped over his shoulder. "What happened to you, son? Did you have a wreck in that old truck of yours?"

He grabbed on to her with his free hand and smiled up at her. "No, Mama, I'll tell you about it later. Right now, I'd like to get in the house, but I have a problem." He gestured toward his right pant leg, the one Dina had slit to above his knee. "My leg's hurt, too. I can't walk."

He was glad when Dina hopped out of the car and hurried around to join them. "Mama, this is Dina. She's a nurse. She was nice enough to drive me here. She's gonna stay with us for a while and help me get started on my physical therapy."

"If that's okay with you," Dina hastened to add. "I don't want to be a bother."

His mother gave her hand a shake. "Of course it's okay with me. Welcome, girl. We always have room for visitors."

"I have a wheelchair in the trunk, but we may need someone else to help lift him into it."

"Stay right here. I'll call my neighbor. As if he doesn't have enough to do on his own place, Brian's been helping with the chores since Will's been gone, but his boys have been helping him, so he hasn't minded. Will's covered for him quite a few times."

The two watched as his mother hurried back into the house. In a matter of minutes, Brian Canter, who lived on the adjoining ranch, was there to assist. A big, strong man, he literally scooped Will into his arms and into the chair, then pulled it up the porch steps as it if weighed not much more than a feather. Brian even went into the bathroom to assist Will before lifting him on to his bed.

As soon as he was gone, Mrs. Martin seated herself beside Will and began stroking his hand. "Tell me, son, what happened to you, and where have you been so long? Why didn't you call me?"

Dina placed a reassuring hand on Will's shoulder. "You and your mom need some private time together. I'll get our things out of the car and bring them inside."

The last thing she heard before she stepped out onto the porch was Will's mother yelling out, "You've been riding bulls? After I told you that you had to stop?"

After everything had been unloaded, Dina wandered into the kitchen, poured herself a glass of iced tea, then moved out onto the porch. She settled herself in one of the rocking chairs and sat gazing out over the pasture, watching brilliant orange and red streaks from the sun decorate the cloudless blue sky above the trees, listening to the twittering of birds somewhere off in the distance, and worrying about the conversation going on inside the house.

Thirty minutes later, Mrs. Martin joined her, her eyes red and rimmed with dark circles. "William told me all the things you've done for him and how you stayed by his side in the hospital. Thank you for being so good to my boy, Dina. He's the best thing that ever happened to me. I just feel bad that I forbade him to ride those bulls like he was some little kid. He's a grown man, old enough, and certainly capable enough of making his own decisions. As his mother, I could give him my opinions, but I had no business *telling* him what he could and couldn't do, much less forbidding him."

"He's a great guy. Your son loves you very much. He never meant to hurt you. You know that, don't you?"

She nodded. "Yeah, I do. I would have lost this ranch without him. Oh, I was upset with him, and wanted to wring his neck for what he'd done, but I'm just glad to have him home. Do you think he'll ever have full use of his arm again? And be able to walk?"

Dina nodded. "With a lot of work, yes, I'm sure he will. And I'm going to do all I can to help him. Within a few days he should be able to get around by himself. His arm and shoulder sustained the worst damage. They'll take a little longer to heal but, hopefully, he'll regain full use of those, too."

Mrs. Martin slid into a rocking chair next to her, her face suddenly taking on a look of pure joy. "I'm so glad you were there for my William. He's sure God sent you to be with him."

"It is kind of uncanny the way we met out on the road that day and then again in Cheyenne. When things like that happen, it's hard to believe God wasn't in it."

"You got anyone waiting for you back in Omaha?"

Dina wrinkled up her forehead. "You mean like. . .a boyfriend?"

The woman nodded.

"Occasionally I date one or two guys I work with at the hospital, but none seriously. Why?"

His mother gave her a mischievous smile. "Just curious."

"I don't know if Will told you but I was raised on a ranch. I'll be happy to assist around here in any way I can. And I'm not much of a cook but I'd like to help with meals, laundry, cleaning, and anything else I can do while I'm here. Is there any chance one of your other sons can come and help with the ranch work until Will can take over again?"

She shook her head. "They might be able to come a few weekends and help out, but you know how it is when you have job and school commitments. It's tough to get away, but they help when they can. All my children enjoy being here but none of them love this old ranch the way my William does."

"Hey!" a male voice rang out from inside the house. "What are you two talking about out there? Come in here where I can hear you!"

The two women laughed then exchanged glances and headed for his room.

"I like your mom," she told him later as she carried his supper tray in to him.

"And she likes having you here. She told me so." He sniffed the air. "Umm, ham. No one fixes it like my mama."

She placed the tray on his lap then hurried back into the kitchen to get her own tray before seating herself in the chair his mother had placed beside the bed. "I really like being here. This place is magical."

He gave her a sideways grin as he unfolded his napkin and placed it beneath his chin. "I love this place but I never thought of it as magical."

"It's like stepping back in time with all the wonderful antique furniture, the heavily starched crocheted doilies, old dishes, that marvelous grandfather clock chiming every hour, the magnificent stairway, the fretwork—all of it. I feel like I've walked into a storybook." She gestured toward his food. "Let's go ahead and pray. We don't want it to get cold."

She remained quiet while he bowed his head and prayed a simple prayer. When he finished, he picked up his fork and speared a piece of the sugar-cured ham his mother had cut into small pieces for him. "Most of what you see around here belonged to my grandparents. Other than adding a few of her own touches, Mom has kept everything pretty much as they left it."

"That's wonderful. So many people get rid of old things,

preferring to have the latest and the newest. Not me. I'd love to have a house just like this one and filled with furniture this lovely." She ran her fingers over the heavily carved rose pattern on the front of his nightstand, taking time to feel each indentation. "They don't make things like this anymore."

He glanced around the room. "I know. I've refinished a few things for Mom. Unlike what you find on the market today, this furniture was built to last."

She sighed. "It breaks my heart when I go to a yard sale or a flea market and see the way people get rid of things they should value."

He speared another piece of ham then gazed at her. "Did Mom have you put your things in that pink room?"

She nodded. "Yes, it's beautiful, and that quilt on the bed—well, I've never seen anything like it. I can hardly wait to crawl under it tonight. Everything about this house is amazing."

"You're not just saying that to be polite?"

"No! It is amazing. I just wish I'd brought my camera so I could get some pictures to take home with me."

"You will stay the whole two weeks, won't you?"

"If necessary, but we need to find you a physical therapist before I go. I'm going to check with the hospital in McCook and see if they know of one who lives nearby." She offered a hearty laugh. "You may be wishing for someone other than me. I'm a pretty tough taskmaster."

"I'm going to do everything you say, Dina. I really appreciate your doing this for me."

She gave his hand a pat. "I'm impressed by how brave you've been through all of this. The pain you've gone through has had to be nearly unbearable yet you've never complained."

"Nothing I can't take. Injuries come with the territory when a guy rides bulls. But God answered prayer. And He not only kept me alive, He sent you to me. What more could I ask?"

She snapped her fingers with a loud snap. "I nearly forgot. Your mom told me Brian Canter was coming over as soon as he finished his chores. He thought you might like to sit in the wheelchair for a while, to change your position."

Will stretched out his good leg. "He's right about that. Though I've only been in this bed for a few hours, it feels like I've been here for days." He popped a cherry tomato into his mouth then smiled at her. "Can I talk you into going out on the porch with me? There's nothing prettier than seeing a Nebraska sunset."

She treated him to her best demure smile. "Why, sir, I'd be honored to sit a spell on the porch with you."

They had no more than finished their supper when Brian appeared at the door. "Ready?" he asked as he pushed the wheelchair close to the bed.

Will nodded. "Oh, yeah. I got a date with this pretty little gal to watch the sunset."

Dina grinned as she picked up their trays and headed for the kitchen. "I'm going to do the dishes for your mom then I'll meet you on the porch."

❧

Will watched her go. He still couldn't believe she had not only driven him home, she was actually going to stay with him for the next two weeks.

"How'd an ugly guy like you snag a beautiful woman like that?" Brian asked as he lifted Will and lowered him into the chair. "What'd you do? Lie to her and tell her there's oil in *them thar* hills?"

Will groaned as he lowered his injured leg onto the footrest. "She is beautiful, isn't she?"

"And nice," Brian added. "If I was you I'd hogtie that little gal and never let her go."

"I'd like to do that very thing, but she's got a great job in

Omaha with a brilliant future ahead of her. What have I got to offer her?"

"A nice home and the love of a good man. Isn't that what most women want?"

He shrugged. "Dina was raised on a ranch, but she's a city gal now. I doubt she'd be interested in living out here where it's so isolated."

Brian pushed the wheelchair toward the bathroom. "Take it from me. I'd say from the way she looks at you, she just might be more interested in you than you think."

Will rolled his eyes. "I wish!"

❧

Dina was already sitting in one of the rocking chairs and staring at the sky when he rolled up beside her. "Look!" she said turning and pointing toward the horizon. "Did you ever see anything so magnificent? It's like God took a paintbrush and generously spread stroke after stroke of red, purple, and orange across His blue sky canvas."

"It's magnificent all right."

"What a beautiful picture that would make. We have some extraordinary sunsets in Omaha, but none the equal of that one."

"Our western Nebraska rainbows are great, too."

"I love rainbows!"

"Maybe you'll get to see one while you're here. Brian said we're supposed to have rain. We could sure use it. Things are really dry."

She turned her attention to him. "You really love this place, don't you?"

"Sure do. Wouldn't want to live any other place. How about you? You really like living in Omaha?"

"Yes, I guess so. It's a nice, friendly city. I like my job and my church. And I like my apartment."

"But if you could live wherever you wanted, would it be Omaha?"

"There are dozens of places I'd like to visit but. . ." She paused and stared off in the distance. "But Nebraska is home to me, and there's no place like home."

"I guess a big city like Omaha has its advantages."

She nodded. "Oh, yes. Omaha is large enough to have everything you want, yet small enough that all of those things are easily accessible. But don't get me wrong. I like living in a big city but I also miss the life I had growing up on our ranch."

"Really?"

"Oh, yes. I hadn't realized how much I'd missed it until I came here with you. Being out in the country again, smelling the fresh, clean air, listening to the mooing of the cattle, hearing the neighing of your horses, even seeing your chickens run free, brings back memories of the wonderful years I spent on my parents' ranch."

"That's good news. I was afraid you'd get bored, living isolated out here for two weeks."

Her eyes widened. "Bored? No way! I'm going to enjoy every minute of it."

"You said you were a barrel racer. I wish I could take you horseback riding."

"I'd like that. Maybe I can stop by the next time I come to visit Burgandi."

They visited, laughing and talking like old friends until Brian appeared. "Your mom and I got most of her chores done. I told her I'd be back early in the morning to help you get out of bed. You ready to call it a night?"

Although he'd rather stay on the porch with Dina, he nodded.

"It's such a beautiful evening, I think I'll stay out here a bit longer. I'll look in on you later," she told him as Brian rolled him toward the door.

Oh, how he wished he could stay out there with her, but he was grateful for Brian's willingness to help him do what he couldn't do for himself.

"You'd better get a good night's sleep," she told him when she stopped by his room as promised. "I'll be putting you through your physical therapy paces in the morning and I'm not going to be easy on you."

"How soon do you think I can start using this leg? I hate being helpless."

"As soon as you can put your weight on it."

Her words were music to his ears. Though he'd had other injuries before, he'd never been immobile and he hated it.

Bracing her hands on the edge of his bed, she leaned over him. "This has been a long, hard day for you. I'm amazed at how well you've done."

"Only because you were with me. I can't thank you enough for driving me here and giving up your vacation time to help me."

"I wouldn't be here if I didn't want to be." She bent and gently kissed his cheek. "Now get to sleep. I'll see you in the morning."

He watched her until the door closed behind her then sighed. She truly was an angel sent from God.

ten

After nearly three intense hours of physical therapy the next morning, Dina gave her head a shake. "Will, you can't expect to get back on your feet after only one session of physical therapy."

He turned his face away with a groan. "But I feel so helpless." He slammed his good fist on the table in frustration. "You're giving up your vacation to be here, I'm causing extra work for my mom, and Brian is taking time away from his own chores to help with mine."

Dina slipped her arm about his shoulders. "Your situation is only temporary. Before long, you'll be back to where you were before this happened. You have to have faith, Will. God is able to heal you."

Blinking, he locked his gaze on the ceiling. "He could also have protected me."

"Do you love the Lord?"

"Of course I do. You know that."

"Then you have to have faith. He had a purpose in it or He wouldn't have allowed it to happen."

He snorted then lifted his bad arm. "What good could come out of it?"

"You won the prize money."

"Which probably won't even pay my doctor and hospital bills."

She playfully tapped his nose with the tip of her finger. "You and I met. I think that's good."

He reached up and grabbed hold of her hand. "Is it?

Do you really think it's good? I've caused you nothing but trouble."

Smiling, she tightened her fingers about his hand. "A little inconvenience maybe, but certainly not trouble. Like I said, I like being here with you, and I like being here on your ranch."

He pulled her hand to his lips and kissed it. "I'm sorry for being such a dork, but most of my life I have been the one taking care of others. I'm not used to having someone take care of me. Have patience with me, Dina. You're the last person on earth I want to upset with my ravings and carrying on."

"I'm not upset *with* you, Will. I'm upset *for* you. I know how hard this has to be but you will get back to normal. Things like this take time and effort. There are no shortcuts but it will happen." Then cuffing his chin with her free hand, she smiled at him. "Trust me. I'm a professional."

"You two ready for lunch?" his mother's voice sounded from the kitchen. "William's favorite. Fried chicken and corn on the cob."

He grinned at Dina. "Yeah, Mom. We'll be right there."

Dina smacked her lips. "Yummy. I love fried chicken." Turning loose of his hand and grabbing on to the handles on his wheelchair, she pushed him into the kitchen. "I hadn't realized you were going to have lunch this early. I should have helped you with it," she told his mother.

Mrs. Martin motioned her toward a chair. "Cooking's my job. Your job is getting that boy of mine back to where he was before—"

Will lifted his hand to silence her. "Now, Mom, no more of that. I did what you didn't want me to do and I'm paying the price. Can we just forget about it?"

His mother leaned over him and gave him a hug. "Yes, my precious son, we'll forget about it. But if you ever do that—"

"Mom!"

She lifted her hands in surrender fashion and backed away. "Okay, 'nough said. I'll keep quiet. I'm just thankful you're home. Let's enjoy our lunch."

Dina ate until she could eat no more then leaned back in her chair with a groan. "I'm stuffed. I can't remember the last time I had home-raised, free-range fried chicken and homegrown corn on the cob. You are a wonderful cook, Mrs. Martin."

The woman laughed. "Not much you can do to fried chicken and corn on the cob to ruin them, but I'm glad you enjoyed it."

"Wait'll you taste her rhubarb pie," Will inserted while reaching for another chicken leg. "It's the best I've ever tasted."

"Don't listen to him. He's biased." Mrs. Martin smiled at her son then passed him the gravy bowl. "Do you like to cook, Dina?"

"I like to, and I used to help my mom, but I don't do it often. It's no fun to cook for one."

"You plan on rising to the top of your profession or do you want to get married and have a family someday?"

Dina sent a nervous glance toward Will. "I guess that depends on when and if I find my Mr. Right. I love my job but I really do want to have a family. I've always felt being a wife and mother is one of God's highest callings."

"And, take it from me, it is." Mrs. Martin lowered her eyes and smoothed at her apron. "But I didn't do too well in the wife department. Will may have told you my husband ran out on us when he was twelve, but I like to think I've done a pretty good job at being a mother."

He reached across the table and took his mother's hand. "Good job? You've been the best mom in the world."

Mrs. Martin dabbed at her eyes with the tip of her apron hem. "And, despite the fact that you go against your mother's wishes sometimes, you're the best son a mother could ask for."

Watching that loving scene play out between Will and his mother touched Dina's heart so deeply she wanted to cry. From the time she'd been a little girl, her grandmother had told her if she wanted to see how a man would treat his wife all she had to do was watch how he treated his mother.

The three startled when the doorbell rang. It was Brian. "I've come to see if you need any help getting in or out of your chair before I go to town for some tractor parts."

Will sent him a grateful smile. "Yeah, I do. Thanks."

❧

An hour later, after Dina had convinced Mrs. Martin to let her run the sweeper and dust, she and Will began their second therapy session.

"Higher. Take it slowly but lift that arm higher," she told him, holding his elbow and adding a bit more pressure.

"Ouch, that hurts."

"Come on, macho man. No pain, no gain—remember?" She watched as he swallowed hard, making his Adam's apple rise and fall. "I know it hurts but it has to be done."

He closed his eyes and gritted his teeth. "If I don't want you to think I'm a sissy, I guess I'd better keep my mouth shut and just do it."

"No, you tell me when if it hurts too much. I need to know when we get to that point so we can stop. Then the next time we do it, it will be a little easier. We don't want to push it too far at a time."

"When can I try to stand on my leg?"

She glanced down at his footrest. "We could try it now but it might be a good idea if we wait until after supper when Brian comes back from helping your mom with the chores. I don't want you falling."

"How soon do you think I can get rid of this chair?"

"Maybe in a couple of days. Thankfully, your leg didn't suffer nearly as much damage as your shoulder and arm." She jabbed at his good shoulder playfully. "Now, enough of this idle chitchat. Lift that arm again."

After a nice supper of homemade vegetable soup made with mostly vegetables from their garden, Dina and Will moved out onto the porch to once again watch the sunset. "You did great today," she told him, reaching over to pat his hand. "I'm proud of you."

He grinned the sideways grin she was beginning to love. "I'm proud of me, too. Boy, you are one tough therapist."

"Oh, that reminds me. While you were resting this afternoon, one of the administrators at the hospital in McCook returned my call with the name of a physical therapist that would be interested in working with you. I called her. She said she already has one client in this area, so it would be no problem for her to work with you, too."

His face took on a look of dismay. "Does that mean you're leaving early?"

"I told her I planned to be here for two weeks, which was fine with her. She's ready to take over when I leave. We're lucky to have found someone."

He huffed. "Yeah, lucky."

"You don't sound very enthused. You do want to get well, don't you?"

"Yeah, sure I do, I just—well—I don't want you to leave."

"I can't stay indefinitely. I have a life to get back to."

He nodded. "I know, but I like having you here."

"And I like being here, but we both knew when I came this was to be a temporary thing."

"Yeah, but I was hoping. . ."

"Hoping what?"

"I don't know. I guess that you'd—never mind. It was a stupid thought."

"Come on. Tell me."

"Naw. Forget it."

"Okay, I'm finished with the chores," Brian's deep voice boomed out as he climbed up the stairs to the porch. "You ready to try to get out of that chair?"

Will sent a quick glance Dina's way. "I am if she is."

Both upset and disappointed that she and Will hadn't had a chance to finish their conversation, Dina hurried to his side. "Brian, I'll hold his good arm to stabilize him while you lift him from behind."

Brian moved into position. "Okay, I'm ready. Go ahead, William. See if you can stand but take it easy. We don't want you hurting yourself."

"Brian's right. Don't rush it. Let us do the work until you're in a standing position. Then slowly put a little weight onto your right leg. If it hurts too bad, quit, and we can try it again tomorrow."

Will nodded then sucked in a deep breath and held it while they helped him out of the chair and onto his good leg. "Here goes."

Dina tightened her grip. "Slowly. Go slowly."

He cautiously leaned slightly to the right, allowing some of his big body weight to shift to that leg then grimaced. "Whoa, I think that's about it."

Dina let out a yelp. "That was great! Before you know it, you'll be walking all over the place."

He looked at her as if she were crazy. "Great? I barely put any weight on it!"

"But it's your first time," she countered, still smiling. "We'll try it again tomorrow, and the next day and the next day, until you're able to stand alone."

He huffed. "If I'm ever able to stand alone."

Brian frowned as he helped Dina lower him back into the chair. "If? Where's your faith, man?"

Will watched as Dina placed the footrest beneath his foot then leaned back with a heavy sigh. "Sorry, guys. Don't pay any attention to me. I know God is able. I just have to trust Him more."

Dina waited in the living room until after Brian had helped Will with his bathroom tasks and assisted him to bed.

"He's all yours," Brian told her when he joined her. "Sure tough to see him like that. I'm really glad you're here to help him."

"So am I, but he's the one who has to do the work. All I can do is assist him, make sure he does it right, and encourage him."

"He's a very special person. The whole community has been asking about him, wanting to know when they could come and visit him. I've told them to give him a day or two to adjust, and then they can come. I don't think there is a person in or around Belmar that Will hasn't helped in one way or another. I remember when his daddy left. It nearly killed that boy. What kind of father would leave his family like that? Especially on his son's birthday?"

"Did you know his father?"

He shook his head. "Not well. No one around here really knew him except the guys at the pool hall. That's where he spent most of his time. To be honest about it, his family is better off without him. He wasn't much good to them and he was mean to Will's mother, and he sure didn't contribute anything to the family finances or the work around here. If it weren't for Will, the Martin family would have lost this ranch. I've never seen a boy work so hard in my life. I guess that's why I wasn't too surprised when his mother told me he'd been off making money bull riding instead of working for other ranchers like she'd thought he was." He tugged his ball cap lower on his brow. "Well, I'd better get going. I wanna help my boys with a few more chores of my own before I go to bed."

Dina walked him to the door then thanked him for helping with both the chores and Will.

"No thanks necessary. He would have done the same thing for me and probably more. That's what good neighbors are for. By the way, tell Will that my brother and I are going to drive over to near where your friend lives tomorrow, to take a look at some cattle, so you'll need to draw me a map. We'll plan on driving Will's truck back so he can use it when he's ready."

"Oh, Brian, that is so nice of you. I know he will appreciate it. He loves that old truck."

"I'll park it out by the barn and bring the keys by in the morning if it's very late when we get back."

She thanked him again then filled a glass with water, wandered into the hallway, and rapped on Will's door. "Can I come in? I've brought you some water."

"Sure, come on in."

After placing the glass on his nightstand, she stood gazing at him.

"What? Why are you looking at me that way?"

"I had quite a talk with Brian about you."

He rolled his eyes. "Oh, no. I suppose he told you about the time I shattered a window in his barn with my BB gun."

She let out a giggle. "You did that?"

"Yeah, though I'm not very proud of it. I had no idea that thing would shoot that far."

"Well, you can relax. That's not what he said. He told me how you'd helped practically everyone in the community with one job or another. How did you find time to do all of that when you were taking care of this ranch?"

"A guy always has time to help his friends."

"You"—she paused to point her finger in his direction—"are amazing. Little did I know when I met you out on that deserted road and was almost afraid of you, that you were such a kind, caring, helpful man, with a boundless love for his family and friends. It's an honor to know you."

"Pshaw. Any guy worth his salt would do the same thing."

"Your father didn't."

"My father wasn't like most men I know, and he sure wasn't worth his salt."

She glanced at the clock on his nightstand then gave his arm a slight pinch. "Brian will be here bright and early and I have a grueling day of therapy planned for you."

He grinned at her. "Don't remind me. You about killed me today."

"If you think that was bad. . ."

He grabbed on to her arm and pulled her close. "No problem. I'm determined to take whatever you can dish out."

Dina felt her pulse quicken as she stared into his blue, blue eyes. "I was hoping you'd say that. Trust me, Will. You'll be back on your feet in no time." She hesitated for a moment then bent and kissed his cheek. "Sleep well. I'll see you in the morning."

He tugged on her hand, drawing her so close it made her feel giddy, and for a brief second she thought he was going to kiss her.

But he didn't.

"Good night, Dina. You're the prettiest thing that has ever happened to me."

Dina lay in her bed staring out the window at the moon for a long time before falling asleep. Being surrounded by the amazing antique furniture and pictures that had belonged to Mrs. Martin's grandparents *was* like taking a step back in time.

There was something magical about being at the Martin ranch and she liked the feeling. Though she needed to get back to work, she almost hated the idea of returning to the city and its rush and hubbub. No wonder Burgandi and her family liked living where they did.

She flipped onto her side and pulled the quilt up about her, a quilt Will's grandmother had made. Though it was old and slightly tattered, it smelled nice, like fabric softener. The last thing she remembered before drifting off was the sound of a turtledove cooing in the tree next to her window.

❧

Friday went pretty much the same as Dina worked with Will on his therapy and assisted his mother in the kitchen. Several neighbors and friends dropped by, bringing him flowers from their gardens, some brought casseroles, while others even stayed to help Brian with the chores.

"I'm going to run into town and pick up a few items I need and do a little grocery shopping for your mom," she told him Saturday morning after they'd finished their therapy session. "Anything you need?"

"Nothing. Just make sure you come back."

She gave him a coy smile. "Wild horses couldn't drag me away."

Though the little town of Belmar didn't offer much in the way of shopping other than groceries, she found almost everything she needed at the local mercantile store, buying a new pair of jeans and a couple of T-shirts for herself, a darling pink apron for Mrs. Martin, and a nice leather wallet for Will to replace the worn one she'd gotten out of his truck for him when they had been in Cheyenne.

Once she got back to the ranch and walked into the house, her arms loaded with groceries, and took one glance at Will, a shiver of delight ran through her.

eleven

She hastily dropped her sacks into a chair as she hurried toward him. "I adore Vandykes. Surely you didn't trim your beard that way by yourself."

"Mom helped. It was pretty tough to do with one hand."

"Well, you both did a terrific job."

She leaned back and sized him up. "You're positively handsome. Now all you need is a little gel to make your hair stand on end like all the guys are wearing it."

"So you like the way my boy looks?" Mrs. Martin said, nodding toward her son as she came in from the kitchen, drying her hands on her apron.

"Absolutely."

Will rolled his eyes. "She told me in the hospital I was gorgeous."

Her eyes shining, Mrs. Martin chuckled. "You are!" Then turning to Dina she added, "He wanted to trim his beard into that Vandyke before he goes to church tomorrow. You will go with us, won't you?"

Dina slipped her arm about the woman. "I'm looking forward to it."

"What a nice bunch of friends and neighbors you have here," she told Will as they sat on the porch later that evening, gazing at the moon. "Everyone in town was so friendly."

He reached over, took her hand, and enfolded it in his. "You could stay, you know."

"Live here in Belmar? How would I make a living?"

"I couldn't pay much but I could hire you on as a ranch hand."

She threw back her head with a laugh. "Me, a ranch hand? At any price you wouldn't be getting your money's worth. In fact, I'd probably be a detriment."

"Detriment or not, my offer still stands. You can hire on anytime you're ready."

She playfully chucked him under the chin. "Don't tempt me. I might take you up on it. I love it here on your ranch."

"Or if you'd rather not be a ranch hand, you could marry me and be my wife."

Though she was sure he was only teasing, his words stunned her. "Don't kid about something like that. Marriage is a serious thing."

"What if I was serious?"

She grinned then swatted at his arm. "If I married you, you'd have to move to Omaha. That's where my job and family are."

"I could never leave this ranch."

"And I could never leave Omaha, so you're off the hook. Besides, I could never be married to a man who fights bulls. Of course you could always give it up. Quit the rodeo."

"I can't. You know that."

"Well then I guess that means I'll spend the rest of my life in Omaha." She rose and stretched her arms. "I hate to end this evening so early but I have to take a shower and shampoo my hair if I'm going to look presentable for church tomorrow morning. Brian said for you to call when you're ready to go to bed and he'd come right over. Want me to call him for you on the way to my room?"

He nodded. "Yeah, sure, I'll see you in the morning."

After a leisurely shower, Dina blow-dried her hair then crawled into bed, taking time to read her Bible and pray before settling down for a good night's sleep.

But at four in the morning, she was awakened by a loud crash from somewhere in the house.

twelve

Without even taking time to pull her robe on over her pajamas she leaped out of bed and rushed into the living room, fully expecting to find an intruder had broken down the front door, or at least the wind had knocked off a table lamp and shattered it into many pieces. But nothing looked amiss. Everything in the living room appeared to be the same as when she had gone to bed.

"What's going on? What was that awful noise?"

Dina spun around to face Mrs. Martin. "I don't know. I thought someone was trying to break in—"

The two women turned as a low groan sounded from the hallway.

"William?"

Instantly, they rushed down the long hall to Will's room where they found him lying on his back, the bed on one side of him, the upset wheelchair on the other.

Dina dropped to her knees and, looping her hair over her ear, bent close to him. "What happened? Are you all right?"

He closed his eyes and let out another groan. "Yeah, I'm as all right as a one-legged man can be, I guess."

She wrapped her arms around him and held him tight. "I'm so, so sorry."

"How did you get down there on the floor like that, son?"

"I needed to go to the bathroom but I didn't want the two of you trying to lift me, so I tried to get out of bed by myself." He gave a disgusted grunt. "I was managing fairly well until that chair scooted out from under me." He gestured toward the pile of broken glass and the water on the floor. "Sorry, Mom, my arm must have hit the water pitcher you'd brought me when I fell."

Dina freed one hand and stroked his forehead. "You poor thing. You should have called us. Your mom and I would have been happy to help you."

He inflated his cheeks then slowly let out a breath of air. "I'm too big for you two to handle."

"We might not have been able to lift you but we could have kept you from falling." She bent and began picking up the glass and depositing it in the small wicker wastebasket they'd set beside his bed.

"Dina's right, son. You should never have tried to get out of bed alone. Are you sure you didn't hurt yourself?"

He lifted his good arm and gave her a half smile. "Other than what will probably be a pretty nifty bruise on my elbow where I banged it on the chair on my way down, the only other injured thing is my pride."

Dina carefully examined his elbow. "You're lucky that's all that was hurt. The way it sounded when you and that chair hit the floor, I thought someone had kicked in the front door."

He glanced down at the water spots on his pajama legs. "I must look like a real doofus."

"You don't look like a doofus to me." Dina tossed the last bit of glass into the wastebasket then stooped down and wrapped her arms around Will. "I have patients who do far more bizarre things than trying to get out of bed by themselves. If I would have been stuck in a bed like you have and needed to get up during the night, I would have done the same thing." She glanced about the room. "Where'd your mom go?"

He shrugged. "I don't know. She was here a second ago."

"Maybe she went to get you another pitcher of water."

"Water is the last thing I need right now."

A shy grin tilted at her lips. "Oh, yeah. I guess it is."

His mother came into the room, carrying a pair of his freshly laundered pajamas. "Brian will be right here."

Will wrinkled up his face and groaned again. "Aw, Mama, why'd you go and do that? It's the middle of the night."

She bustled about the room, straightening his bed and making neat little piles out of his things on the nightstand. "Brian told me to call him anytime you needed help. He didn't care what time it was. I only did as I was told."

"She's right, Will. I heard him tell her that very thing," she said in Mrs. Martin's defense.

"Thanks for leaving the front door open for me." Three sets of eyes turned as Brian came into the room, unshaven and his hair all askew. "I'm glad you called me."

Will huffed. "Mama shouldn't have called you. You need your sleep."

Brian bent and gently cuffed Will's bicep with his fist. "You tryin' to tell me you wouldn't do the same for me?"

He shrugged. "You know I would."

Brian gave him a wink. "Case closed. You call me anytime you need help, William. I mean that." Then turning to the women, he motioned toward the door. "Why don't you gals give us men a little privacy?"

"Ah, sure." Dina grabbed on to Mrs. Martin's hand as the two walked out of the room. Once they were out of earshot she said, "It really scared me when I heard that crash but I never dreamed it was your son."

"Me neither, but knowing how stubborn he can be, I shouldn't have been surprised. I just praise God all he got out of it was a bruised elbow."

Dina led her to her room. "You need your rest. Go back to bed. I'll stay up until Brian leaves and make sure the door is locked." She was relieved when Mrs. Martin didn't protest and went right to bed. She sat on the sofa, leafing through a magazine until Brian appeared.

"We got him changed into dry pajamas and he's back in bed now. I'm goin' home. I'll be back in the morning, probably about seven."

Dina thanked him and locked the door then headed for her room, but on impulse she paused at Will's door.

"I'm awake. Come on in."

She stepped inside then flipped on his bedside lamp before seating herself in his righted wheelchair. "Are you sure you didn't get hurt? From the sound of it, you had quite a fall."

"No, I'm okay. You know, I think I could have made it if that chair hadn't rolled out from under me. I thought I could get in it without setting the brake but I know better now."

"We can work on it after we get home from church. You're getting stronger every day. Since you can stand on one leg, with a little practice I'll bet you can get yourself in and out of that wheelchair."

His face took on a slight smile and he almost looked happy. "You really think so? That would sure make me feel more like a man instead of—what I am now."

"I not only think so—with your determination—I know so." When he reached out his hand she took it and cradled it in hers. Then grinning, she added, "Take it from me, even in that wheelchair, you're very much a man."

"Thanks, Dina. After my falling fiasco, I needed the encouragement. I can't tell you how embarrassed I was to have you and my mom find me splattered all over the floor like a helpless baby."

She rose and kissed his cheek. "You, my big, strong man, are anything but a helpless baby. Now get some sleep. I'll see you in the morning."

❧

To Dina's surprise, the little country church was filled to near capacity when they entered its sanctuary the next morning. And as expected, everyone flooded around Will, warmly greeting him and asking how he was doing. She smiled and nodded as he introduced her to each one, honestly saying how nice it was to meet them and how glad she was to be in Belmar. "It must be rewarding to have so many friends," she told him as the organ sounded and everyone moved toward their places. Grinning, she grasped the handles of his chair. "You'll have to fill me in on the protocol. Do we sit just anywhere or do you have a special pew?"

He gestured toward the second row on the right. "That one right there but it might be a good idea if we sat in the back. I don't want to be in anyone's way and I sure don't want to block their view."

The music was far more than she had expected. A young couple did a marvelous job, singing a duet; and an older woman's solo, which Dina could tell came right from the heart, was one of the best she'd ever heard. Even the congregational singing was superb. "You've got a great voice," she whispered to Will as the pastor moved to the pulpit to deliver his message.

He grabbed her hand and gave it a squeeze. "Funny you should mention that. I was going to tell you the same thing."

Though she wondered what people would think when the two of them held hands during the entire message, she made no effort to pull away. She liked holding hands with him. It made her feel secure, safe, and yes—warm and fuzzy.

"So what did you think of our little church?" he asked as the two sat in the living room after a delicious dinner of barbecued brisket and baked potatoes.

"I liked it. Everyone made me feel right at home. Your mom

told me four generations of your family have attended Belmar Community Church. Did your dad ever go to church with you?"

He responded with a disgusted grunt. "My dad go to church? Not on your life. He even tried to keep Mom and us kids from going."

"That's too bad."

"Speaking of dads, you promised you'd tell me your story but you never did. How about now?"

She blanched. "You sure you want to hear it?"

"Dina, I want to know everything about you, both the good and the bad."

After propping her foot up on the footstool, she leaned toward him. "Like you, my father was a bull rider."

His eyes widened. "He was? Why didn't you tell me?"

"And like you," she went on, preferring to leave his questions unanswered until he'd heard her story, "despite sustaining a number of injuries, he kept riding, totally ignoring the pleading by those of us who loved him and begged him to quit while he was ahead. Eventually, he was gored by a bull, Will, badly gored—bad enough that he spends all his days and evenings in his wheelchair. The only way he can get out is by using a sling-type apparatus, and even then my mom has to operate it for him. With his back problems, he can't do it by himself. The man will never walk again. He's turned into a vindictive, demanding old man, expecting my mom to come at his beck and call and wait on him like she's his servant."

Will shook his head. "No wonder you're so against bull riding."

"He's the reason I quit barrel racing. Even though I enjoyed it and got pretty good at it, even barrel racing has its injuries. I couldn't stand the idea of someone having to take care of me like that. That's why it is so hard for me to believe you'd go back to it."

"I have to, Dina. It's the only way I can make that kind of money."

"But you said you'd have this place paid off in a year."

"And I will, but I don't want to live with my mom all my life. I'd like to build a house down by the creek and have a family. Families cost money."

"Are you and your dad on good terms?" he asked as if wanting to move the conversation back to her father instead of trying to explain himself.

"Not really. When I go visit my mother, he and I don't even speak to each other. I hate him for the way he treats her. He wears his injuries like a badge of honor for bravery."

"I guess we have more in common than we'd realized. We both hate our fathers."

"Yeah, I guess we do." On impulse, she jumped to her feet. "Let's forget about our dads. We have work to do. You need to start trying to put more weight on your leg. Other than being badly bruised and painful from your run-in with that bull, there's really nothing wrong with it. You've already been able to put some weight on it. Remember Dr. Flaming said you should start trying to take steps and walk on it as soon as you felt like trying it."

"Sounds good to me."

"Then let's give it a try. Back your chair up against the wall so it can't roll out from under you." After he did as instructed she bent and locked the wheels then reached out to him. "Grab my hand with your good hand and try to pull yourself up like we've been practicing but keep the weight on your good leg until you're on your feet."

"I weigh too much. Maybe we should wait for Brian. You'll never be able to hold me."

"If I can't, we'll wait for Brian."

He locked his good hand with hers and slowly pulled

himself to a standing position, groaning with each inch as he moved. "I did it!"

"See, I told you I could hold you."

"I wish I could use a crutch."

"Impossible, with that shoulder. Don't even think about it. Wrap your arm around my shoulders and lean on me. You doing okay?"

"With you holding me up I am."

She looped her arm around his waist. "Now shift some of your weight over to your injured leg and then try to take a step."

He winced then sucked in an exaggerated breath. "Wow, the muscles in my calf feel like they're about to explode."

"And they will for a while but it'll get better. Let's try another step but keep it small."

"Yes, boss."

Her arm still looped around his waist, they moved in sync as he took one, then two more small hobbling steps, his face contorting each time he shifted his weight from one foot to the other.

"Good job. Would you like to sit on the sofa for a while?"

He bobbed his head. "Yes, but let me walk there."

"It's too far."

"Let me try."

"Okay, but keep leaning on me. I don't want you to fall."

"Hey, I like this. I've been wanting an excuse to hold you in my arms." He grinned. "Correction—arm—singular."

"I like it, too, but you'd better quit joking and concentrate on staying on your feet."

Although it was a bit of a struggle for him to make it and get seated, he finally did. "Maybe Brian won't have to come over and help me anymore."

She sat down beside him. "You're doing great but let's not

rush things. By the time I have to leave. . ."

He quickly held up his hand to silence her. "Don't even mention it. I can't imagine my life without you."

"Your new therapist will probably do a better job with you than I'm doing!"

"I'm not talking about my therapy, Dina, I'm talking about you. You've become part of my life."

"And you've become part of mine, a very pleasant part, but life goes on."

He shrugged. "Yeah, I guess you're right, but you won't forget me? You will keep in touch?"

"You know I will. And when I come to western Nebraska to visit Burgandi, I'll plan on leaving early enough to stop here on my way to say hello, that is unless you're off somewhere riding bulls."

They sat on the sofa for another hour or so, laughing and talking, enjoying one another's company, and sharing stories of their high school times. When his mother came home from visiting one of the neighbors, she and Dina helped him back into the bedroom so he could stretch out awhile before supper.

"You have a wonderful son," she told Mrs. Martin later as they stood side by side doing the supper dishes.

"He thinks you're pretty wonderful, too."

She finished drying a bowl then placed it on the shelf. "Only because I offered to drive him home and help with his therapy."

"I'd say it's much more than that. He's sure gonna miss you when you're gone. So am I. You've been a real blessing to this family."

"I hope so. That's the reason I came."

"Dina!"

She turned at the sound of Will's voice. "I'm in the kitchen!"

"Can you come and help me? I'd like to go out on the

porch for a while."

Mrs. Martin took the towel from her hands. "Go on. I'll finish here."

By the time she reached his room, he had already slipped his feet into his loafers and was ready to stand.

"Put your arm around me."

A mischievous smile curled at his lips. "Be glad to."

She gave him a playful nudge. "You're pretty frisky tonight."

"Probably because I can finally get out of that bed without Brian's help. I'm not used to depending on other people. Usually I'm the one who does the helping."

"So I've heard."

"From Mom and Brian, right?"

"Uh-huh, and your pastor, and some of the ladies I met at your church. Shall I go on?"

"They're all exaggerating."

"What about me? You helped me. Remember?"

He tightened his arm about her shoulders. "Only because you were so cute. If you'd been ugly I would have turned my truck around and gotten out of there fast."

"You know that's not true. You'd help anyone in distress."

He groaned as he lowered himself into the old metal porch glider. "Yeah, I guess I would. Like the Bible says, it sure is better to give than to receive. I'd much rather help than be helped."

When she sat down and scooted up close beside him, he slipped his good arm around her. "Thanks, Dina."

"For what?"

"Everything. Staying by my side in the hospital, encouraging me, driving me here, giving up your vacation to help with me—but mostly—for just being here. As big a mess as I'd gotten myself into, I'm not sure I could have made it without you."

"Sure you could. You're a fighter."

"I always thought I was, but I'd never been injured this badly."

"You're going to come through this as good as new. You know that, don't you?"

"I'm hoping so but. . ." He paused.

A chill of excitement ran through her when he smiled down at her.

"Dina, what would you do if I tried to kiss you?"

With the beat of her heart quickening, she gave him a blank stare. "I—I don't know."

"Would you shove me away?"

"I—don't think so." She held her breath as he drew closer and closer.

"Would you slap me?" His voice was a mere whisper.

"Ah—probably not." Her toes curled up as his lips feathered against hers.

"Would you be upset with me?"

"No."

Dina felt light-headed, dizzy, as his lips claimed hers in a slow, almost childlike kiss.

"Wow, that was nice!" he murmured as their lips parted.

Not sure what to do or say, she simply gazed into his beautiful eyes and nodded.

Then, without asking permission, he kissed her again. And this time, instead of sitting like a concrete statue, she participated. A feeling of giddiness came over her as she cupped his cheek with her hand and pressed her lips to his. She had kissed a few of the guys she had seriously dated but none of those kisses had made her heart flutter and her head reel like Will's kisses. He kissed her a third time, a fourth, then a fifth before loosening his grip on her.

Reluctantly, she pulled away and gave him a shy smile.

"I think it's time we call it a day. You need your rest. I'm planning on taking you through at least four therapy sessions tomorrow."

"Can we make it three?"

"Three? Did I tire you out too much today?"

"No, but now that I can get around some, I want to have plenty of time to show you the rest of the ranch. I thought we could go horseback riding. That is, if you think you can handle saddling up the horses."

Her jaw dropped. "Sure, I can do that but how—"

"How am I going to get on my horse? Brian offered to help in the morning when he comes over to do the chores. I figured if you could maneuver Goldie up next to the porch, Brian could hang on to me as I throw my bad leg over the saddle and help me get centered."

"Won't it hurt to lift your leg that way?"

"Yeah, I'm sure it will, but I really want to show you around. Is it a date?"

Dina let a big smile burst forth. "It's a date!"

❧

Will grinned over his shoulder at Dina the next morning as they rode through a grove of trees near the creek. "Getting up on Goldie's back was easier than I thought it'd be—thanks to Brian."

She gave her horse's neck a gentle pat. "I've missed having a horse. I'd like to take Silver home with me."

"You think there'd be room for him in your apartment?"

"Maybe, if I took the furniture out, but I doubt he'd be as happy there as he is here in this beautiful place."

He slowed Goldie's pace, giving her time to ride up next to them. "You really like it here?"

"Are you kidding? A person would have to be crazy not to like it."

"The barn and the outbuildings are old, the fences need replacing, the windmill's about to fall down. . . ."

"That's what gives this place charm. I'm amazed you've been able to keep things up as much as you have. Those buildings may be old but they are in such good shape and so well painted. And the windmill? I wish I had a picture of it just the way it is."

He chuckled. "Charm, eh? I never thought of it that way." Tugging on the reins, he brought Goldie to a halt. "Look over there. See those stakes I've driven into the ground? That's where I'd like to build a house. Do all the work myself. Make it really special."

"Oh, Will, what a lovely place for a home. The trees are gorgeous and there's such a great view of the creek."

He gave the reins a gentle flip and Goldie moved forward. "Gotta find me a wife first."

Dina took one last look at the area he'd pointed out. It *was* a beautiful place. The perfect spot for a house, and she found herself envious of the woman who would someday become Will's wife, live there with him, and bear his children.

"You coming?" he called back to her.

"Right behind you."

thirteen

The next week flew by as Dina and Will spent nearly every waking moment together, enjoying one another's company and working to get his arm and shoulder in the best shape possible before she left and his new therapist took over. In addition to their therapy sessions, they'd driven into town, attended a concert in the little city park, visited with friends and neighbors, and even witnessed the wedding of one of Will's high school buddies. She was extremely pleased with his progress, but in some ways she felt like she was running out on a job half done.

"I can't believe this is our last day together," he told her as they rode Goldie and Silver on the winding trail that ran along the creek's edge.

She sighed. "Me, either."

"You've done nothing but work since you've been here. I guess you're looking forward to getting back to your big-city job."

"Yeah, sorta."

"You don't sound very enthused."

"Only because I hate to leave this place—and you."

"You could stay."

Dina huffed. "And do what? I'm a single gal, remember? I have to make a living." She allowed a teasing grin to quirk up her mouth. "And don't tell me again you'd hire me. I'd make a lousy ranch hand."

"You could get a job at Community Hospital over at McCook. It's not that far away. They just built a $3.8-million-dollar rehab center."

"Why would I want to live in McCook? I don't know a soul over there."

"You could live here on the ranch and drive back and forth. We could fix up the old ranch hand's cabin."

"Um, as much as I like it here, I don't think that would be a good idea." She turned to him with an impish grin. "Race you back to the house!" Then before he could take her up on her challenge, she gave Silver's sides a kick and they were off.

"Hey! Not fair!" Will shouted as he and Goldie followed in hot pursuit.

With the wind whipping through her hair, she gave him a wave then called back over her shoulder. "Whoever said life was fair?"

When they got back to the barn Dina applauded as Will dismounted by himself, without her or Brian there to help ease him down. "Good job. I'm so proud of you. You've worked really hard. You're able to walk, ride your horse, and help with some of the chores. Do you realize how far you've come in two weeks?"

He lifted his bad shoulder with a wince. "Yeah, but I still can't use my arm much."

"But you've admitted it's getting better every day. If you continue to work with the therapist and do your exercises regularly like we've been doing, you'll be back to normal before you know it." She reached out for his hand. "Speaking of working with your therapist, we'd better get back to the house and get started on this morning's session."

Mrs. Martin was all smiles two hours later when she greeted them as they entered the kitchen. "Since this is the last time the three of us will have lunch together before you go back to Omaha, I've fixed all your favorites, Dina. Fried chicken, mashed potatoes, pepper gravy, and my sour-cream coleslaw."

Dina lifted the lid on the skillet. "Oh, yummy, that smells wonderful! But you shouldn't have gone to so much trouble."

"After what you've done for my boy, there is nothing I could do to repay you." She gestured toward Will. "Look at him. He'll soon be back to his usual ornery self and we have you to thank for it."

"You give me way too much credit."

"Just remember, Dina. You'll always be welcome in this home. Come as often as you can and stay as long as you like."

She bent and kissed Mrs. Martin. The two had become close friends. It was going to be hard to leave her, too.

"Dina worked me pretty hard this morning," Will told his mom as the two women washed the dishes and cleaned up the kitchen after their sumptuous lunch. "I think I'll go stretch out until she's ready for our afternoon session."

Dina flipped at him with her dish towel. "If you think I worked you hard this morning, wait until you see what I have planned for this afternoon."

He grabbed hold of the towel, yanking it out of her hand, and flipped it back at her. "Bring it on, babe. You don't scare me."

His mother stepped in between them. "You two sound like a couple of kids."

Dina set the last dish on the shelf then closed the cabinet door. "Well, this kid has got to stop her playing and do some packing. I have a long drive ahead of me tomorrow and I want to stop and spend some time with my mom on the way back."

Will let out a grunt. "You that anxious to get away from me?"

She tapped the tip of his nose playfully. "You know better than that, but my time here has come to an end. I have to get back to my job."

❧

Though Dina gathered most of her things from the closet and drawers and placed them in her suitcase, she did it with little enthusiasm. *Come on, girl,* she told herself, trying to sound convincing. *You've done all you can for that man. It's time to get back to Omaha, to your job, your friends, your church, to the life you had there before you came to this ranch. You were happy there, remember?*

She turned and stared at her image in the dresser mirror. "If I was happy living there and had such a great life, why am I so sad about leaving?"

Though she had posed the question, in her heart she already knew the answer.

Will.

❧

Their afternoon session was every bit as vigorous and demanding as she'd promised it would be. Although Will complained about it, she could tell his complaining was nothing more than good-natured kidding and was pleased with how hard he worked.

After a light supper, he disappeared for an hour or so to write some checks and take a quick shower. Dressed in the white peasant-type blouse and the full-tiered denim skirt she'd bought in town on one of their shopping trips, Dina was waiting for him on the porch when he returned. To make her outfit even more festive and memorable for their last night together, she had pulled up one side of her long blond hair and anchored it with a red silk rose. She'd even touched a hint of her favorite perfume behind each ear.

"Um, you smell nice," Will told her as he bent to kiss her cheek before seating himself close beside her in the metal glider. "And you look—beautiful. That's the stuff you bought in town, isn't it?"

"You like it?"

"Yeah, I like it. All I can say is wow!" He slipped his good arm about her shoulders and drew her close. "So you're really going to leave me."

"Yes, I have to."

"I—I don't want you to go."

"I don't want to go but. . ." She held her breath as he lifted her face to his.

"You know I'm crazy about you, don't you?"

"You never told me."

"Only because I didn't think you'd want to hear it. I–I've never felt this way about a woman. You're in my every thought all day and I dream about you at night. Being with you each day and having you so close has been driving me crazy."

Dina found herself nearly speechless. She had felt a real connection between them, but she'd had no idea he cared for her that deeply.

"I've wanted so much to hold you in my arms, smother your sweet face with kisses, and ask you to stay."

"I can't. As much as I'd like to stay here and live in the old cabin, I hate the idea of having to drive back and forth to work every day at the McCook hospital."

"Sweetheart, you don't understand. When I said I wanted to ask you to *stay* with me, I didn't mean as a tenant in our cabin, I meant as my *wife*. I want you to marry me!"

His unexpected words nearly knocked the wind out of her. "Me—marry you?"

"Look, don't get mad at me. I didn't mean to offend you. I know I have nothing to offer. That's why I didn't tell you." He backed away, leaving her sitting with her mouth hanging open. "I should have kept my big mouth shut. Now you *are* mad at me! I love you, Dina, but I know you could never love me."

"But I do love you!" The words slipped out before she could stop them.

He stared at her. "You do?"

"Yes. I've never believed in love at first sight but I think

I've loved you ever since the night I rode with you in the ambulance."

He gave his hands a despairing lift. "The only things I can give you are myself—a broken-down cowboy—and my love. And, someday, this ranch. I can't offer you the glamour and excitement of living in the city and the wealth some other man or maybe one of the doctors you work with can give you. You deserve so much more. I guess I shouldn't be surprised that you'd turn me down."

She grasped the biceps of his good arm with both hands. "But I haven't turned you down."

He shifted around to face her. "You mean you might say yes?"

"I'm thinking about it. The last thing I expected when I came out here on the porch this evening was a proposal." She gave him her most demure smile. "That was a proposal, wasn't it? Or did I only assume it was? You said you *wanted* me to marry you, you didn't exactly *ask* me to marry you."

Using his good hand to brace himself, he struggled to drop to one knee in front of her. "Well, I'm asking you now. Dina Spark, I love you more than my humble words can ever express. Would you marry me? Do me the honor of becoming my wife?"

fourteen

Will's words were the ones she'd longed for but never expected to hear. The kindest, sweetest, most caring, self-sacrificing man she'd ever known was asking her to marry him and spend the rest of her life with him. And best of all, he loved her and he loved her Lord. She was about to say yes and throw her arms about his neck when the sudden image of her father, imprisoned in his wheelchair for life, day after dreary day, with nothing to look forward to but more misery and pain, swept across her mind.

"I want to, Will. Oh, how I want to, but first I need to ask you something. Do you, or do you not, intend to return to bull riding? It's important that I know and I want an honest answer."

When he gazed at her for a moment without answering, something in his eyes told her she already knew what he was going to say.

"I have to, honey. It's the only way I can pay this ranch off," he said, holding tightly to her hand. "One more good season, two at the most, and I'll quit."

She tugged her hand away and swallowed at the lump in her throat. "No! That's not acceptable! What if you were injured again, maybe even gored by a bull like my father was? I can't take that chance, Will. I've seen what his accident has done to my mother, and I've seen what it has done to him. If you don't love me enough to. . ."

He reached out for her but she backed away.

"I do love you and I'd do anything for you—except what

you're asking. Dina, I've worked since I was a kid to make sure this old ranch stayed in our family. I'm within a year or so of seeing all my work pay off. I can't quit now. It's not fair that you even ask."

Her hands went to her hips. "You're a man of God. Where's your faith? Why can't you trust God to meet your financial needs?"

"Trust Him?" he shot back. "Who do you think gave me this talent in the first place? Dina, when life looked the bleakest for my mom and us kids, and like there was no way we could hang on to this place, I won a hundred dollars at a local rodeo, riding bulls. That was enough to keep the banker happy for a while. From that time on, every penny I made at rodeos went to help make those mortgage payments. God gave me the talent for riding bulls. Not only did He give me the talent, He gave me the courage. Facing an angry bull takes courage. Not many men can do it."

"And I can't face being married to a man who does. If you won't give up bull riding, I can't marry you! I'm sorry. That's just the way it is."

"Even if I promise I'll be careful?"

"I'm sure you were being careful the night you rode Gray Ghost. Being careful is not enough."

"Dina, please. See it from my side."

"No! You see it from my side. I refuse to be married to a bull rider! I can't stand the idea that you might end up like my father—or maybe even dead! No! I love you, but I won't marry you, Will, not unless you quit the rodeo now! That's my final word!" With that, she whirled around and ran into the house, into the privacy of her bedroom where she could cry her eyes out.

A few minutes later, she heard his labored footsteps in the hall as he headed toward his room. *Lord*, she cried out from within her heart, *why? Why would You allow me to fall in love with this man, a professional bull rider, when You knew how I always kept my distance from every guy who had anything to do with rodeos? Now here I am, head over heels in love and going home with nothing but wonderful memories and a broken heart.*

When morning came, Dina dragged herself out of bed, tidied up her room, then took a quick shower before dressing and going into the kitchen for breakfast.

"I didn't mean to eavesdrop last night," Mrs. Martin said, standing in front of the range, shifting the sizzling bacon around in the pan, "but you two got pretty loud out there on the porch."

Dina sat down at the table and poured herself a glass of orange juice. "Sorry about that but we had some pretty heavy things to discuss."

"From the way you stormed down the hall when you passed my bedroom, I guess things didn't end well between the two of you."

She sighed. "No, not well at all."

"Morning."

Dina stared into her glass and didn't bother to turn around at the sound of his voice. "Morning."

"Beautiful morning out," his mother inserted cheerfully, as if trying to break the gloom that suddenly engulfed the room.

They both nodded.

Dina glanced at the wall clock then rose. "I–I'm not very hungry. I think I'm going to head on out. I want to stop in Farrell to see my mom and then I'd like to get back to Omaha as soon as possible."

Mrs. Martin laid down her spatula and, wiping her hands on her apron, hurried to Dina's side. "You sure, honey? Breakfast is almost ready."

Dina wrapped her arms about the woman and gave her a

hug. "I'm sure. Thanks for everything. You've been wonderful to me. I'm so glad I got to know you."

Will stood awkwardly to his feet. "I'll—ah—walk you to your car."

"You needn't. I've already taken everything out. I'm ready to go."

"I'll walk with you anyway."

She answered with a slight shrug. "Suit yourself." After she told his mother good-bye, with Will hobbling beside her the two walked silently to her car. When he opened her door for her, she stuck out her hand. "I'd tell you to take care of yourself but I know you won't. Now that I look back on things, I realize I wasted two weeks of my life by staying here and trying to nurse you back to good health since you're planning to go right back and take a chance on the same thing, or something even worse, happening to you again."

He tried to hold on but she pulled her hand away and hurriedly slipped into the driver's seat, inserted the key in the ignition, and gave it a turn.

"Dina, I wish you'd understand."

She yanked on the handle, shutting the door with a slam. "And I wish you'd understand. I love you, Will. I'll always love you—but not as a bull rider."

"Please, sweetheart, we could have such a good life together."

"Yes, we could, but not under your conditions. Good-bye." Before he could say another word, she pressed down on the gas pedal and took off, scattering rocks and gravel at his feet. The last image she had of the love of her life was when, with tear-filled eyes, she glanced into the rearview mirror.

❧

Heartbroken and discouraged, Will watched through the curl of dust stirred up by Dina's tires until her car disappeared up the road. *God, why? Why, when I've prayed so long for a wife who would accept me the way I am and the pressures of life that have fallen upon my shoulders? Why would You bring such a beautiful, caring, Christian woman into my life, let me fall in love with her, just to have her refuse my proposal? All because I can't quit the rodeo like she asked me to. I don't understand.*

Am I wrong to want to pay off this farm and secure it for my mom? Lord, I'm not a learned man like those doctors Dina works with every day. Other than bull riding, I have no talent, no other means in addition to the small amount this ranch brings in, to earn enough to pay off the mortgage. And I wanted so much to build a house for Dina and me, down by the creek in the area we both love. Was that asking too much? Am I being stubborn, Lord? If I had told her I'd quit bull riding, would You have helped me find another way to pay off the ranch?

Show me, Father. Tell me. I need to hear from You. I need to know Your will for my life.

❧

"He actually asked you to marry him?" Dina's mother gasped as the two sat in the kitchen, sipping freshly made coffee. "I could tell by the way you talked about him when you phoned me that you two had grown close, but I had no idea you had fallen in love with the man."

"I knew it all along, Mom. I just wouldn't admit it to myself. It's hard to explain, but Will was everything I could want in a man, and yet he had the one thing in his life I couldn't tolerate." She glanced into the living room to make sure her father wasn't listening before going on. "What if Will was injured again, maybe even gored by a bull like Dad was? What if he became like Dad, arrogant and demanding, and expected me to wait on him and talked to me like Dad does you? I couldn't take it, and I don't know how you can."

"Mary, come in here!" her father bellowed. "I dropped the *TV Guide*. And bring me a cup of coffee when you come, only this time don't put so much cream in it."

Dina grabbed her mother's arm. "Don't do it, Mom. You're not his maid. His chair is electric. Let him come in and get his own coffee."

Her mother pulled away from her grasp. "I don't mind doing it. He's my husband."

"But he abuses you, both physically and verbally. You don't have to take it from him. I worry about you. He's dangerous with that hot temper of his. Someday, he may actually hurt you."

"Dina, your father may be all the things you say he is, and I admit sometimes I get very irritated and hurt by what he says and does, but we have some good times together, too. Our marriage, before he was injured, was wonderful. Remember when our neighbor led me to the Lord not long after your father was hurt? When I confessed my sins, I realized one of my worst sins was bitterness—bitterness toward your father. I asked God to take my life and make it what He wanted it to be. You know, after I prayed that prayer, my love for my husband became stronger than it had been when we'd first married. When I said 'I do' and vowed to love and care for him until death do us part, I meant it. Now, when the bad times come, I remember the good times. I've never doubted God is the One who brought us together. Taking care of your father is my calling in life."

Her mother's words pierced Dina's heart. She finally understood that the reason for her mother staying and caring for her husband was the same reason Will felt God had called him to love and care for the family his father had deserted and left destitute.

That night, as she knelt by her bed, she asked God for forgiveness for her sins. Not for any dreadful sins she had committed but for not acknowledging God's way was always the best way, even though sometimes she didn't understand it or agree with it.

Forgive me, God. Give me a pure heart, she cried out from the deep inside her. *Show me Your will. I'm so confused. Help me, Father God! Help me!* Sobbing as though her heart would break, she wiped at her tears.

"You call Me Father, but what about your earthly father? Can't you find it in your heart to forgive him, even as you ask Me to forgive you?" a small voice from somewhere inside her seemed to say.

Dina stopped sobbing and listened. *God, is that You?*

"It's time to forgive your father and make things right between the two of you," the small voice continued. *"He, too, is having a rough time. He needs his daughter."*

❧

The rest of that evening and far into the night, Dina thought about the last conversation she'd had with Will, as well as the things God had laid upon her heart. She wanted to accept Will's desire to continue riding bulls, but she just couldn't, even though she knew God *could* protect him. Paying off the rest of the farm's mortgage and having enough money to build a house down by the creek were admirable goals, goals that had kept Will working day and night since he had been twelve years old. There had to be another way, other than his winnings, to do what he felt he had to do. But how? *Please, God, show us a way. Will and I love each other and want to be together. Isn't this what You want, too?*

❧

When her cell phone rang at five the next morning, with Will's number showing on Caller ID, she leaped to answer it.

"I couldn't sleep for thinking about you, sweetheart," he told her with a heavy sigh. "We can't let a love like ours die without at least trying to come up with a solution. I've given our situation some serious thought, Dina. I'm giving up bull riding. I—I don't know how I'll manage to pay off the mortgage without the extra money—but I can't live without you."

"Oh, Will, are you sure? As much as I want to marry you, I wouldn't want you to do something you'll regret later and end up hating me for."

"I could never hate you, Dina, for anything. But I'm serious about giving it up. There's no getting around it; bull riding is a dangerous sport. Who knows? Next time I might get hurt even worse. As I lay in bed last night, I weighed out my options. What was more important to me? Paying off the ranch? Or marrying you, the woman I love, and spending the rest of my life as your husband and, hopefully, the father of our children? When I faced those two choices head-on, the decision was easy."

Tears filled her eyes as she gripped the phone. "Honest? You're not just saying that because it's what you know I want to hear?"

"Dina, I'd do anything to have you by my side. Being here at the ranch without you last night, knowing I may never see you again, hold you in my arms, kiss your sweet face—well, it made me just plain sick. Somehow, I'll figure out a way to earn the extra money. I'm a good worker. I can always hire myself out to other ranchers who need help."

"Will, I've been thinking, too. I really wouldn't mind driving back and forth to McCook. With my background and the glowing recommendation I'm sure my supervisor will give me, I know I can land a well-paying job in their new rehab facility. With what I could make at the McCook hospital and what the ranch would bring in, surely we could pay off the mortgage within a year as you planned."

"Driving back and forth to McCook every day could get mighty tiresome, especially in the winter. Southwest Nebraska winter storms can be pretty bad, with lots of snow."

She let loose a nervous giggle as her excitement grew. "Oh? And you think our winters here in Omaha are like the tropics? I could do it, Will. I know I could. That way we could be together. Besides, I have a little money saved up and I still have the savings account my aunt left me."

"We'd have to live with Mama. It might be years before we could get enough money ahead to build our house."

"I love your mom. We got along great while I was there. It's a big house. There's plenty of room for all three of us."

The sudden silence on the other end frightened her. Now that he had come face-to-face with the decision he would have to live with for the rest of his life, was he having second thoughts?

"I know you want me to give up bull riding, sweetheart, and I'm gladly doing it, but I was wondering how you'd feel about me raising bulls for rodeo stock?"

"Oh, Will, I'd be totally happy to see you raise bulls. I know you love the rodeo and, as long as you aren't riding bulls yourself, I might even get to the point that I loved rodeo, too, just because you do."

"Then it's settled?" he asked brightly. "You're accepting my proposal?"

She could almost see his smiling face. "Oh yes, my love! Yes! Yes! Yes!"

❧

"What are you doing here this time of day?" her mother asked the next morning when Dina walked into her kitchen. "It's nearly noon. I thought you had to be back to work this morning."

"I have been to work, Mom. I turned in my resignation."

"What? You're quitting? Why? I thought you loved that job. What are you going to do?"

Dina couldn't contain her joy. "I'm going back to Will! I've accepted his proposal. He's giving up bull riding!"

"You talked to him?"

She threw back her head with a laugh. "Yes! He phoned early this morning. Everything is settled. I'm going to spend the rest of the day packing up my personal items, everything else the movers can pack. I'm heading back to Belmar first thing in the morning."

Her mother sat down at the table, staring at her with wide eyes. "I—I had no idea—"

"Neither did I when I went to bed last night but, believe me, I really prayed things would work out and they have! God is sooo good!"

Mrs. Spark gave her head a shake. "I can't believe it. My little girl is getting married."

"I'll let you know when we decide on a wedding date. I want us to be married in Belmar since that's where we'll be making our home, and I want you and Dad to be there. I had a long talk with God last night." She gave her mother shy grin. "Or should I say God had a talk with me. Because of that I'm making some radical changes in my life and I couldn't be happier." She gestured toward the living room. "Dad in there?"

Her mother nodded. "I was just about to take his lunch to him."

"Could you hold off for a while? I need to talk to him."

"I guess so." She eyed Dina suspiciously. "You're not going to get into another argument with him, are you?"

"No, just the opposite. I'm going to apologize and ask his forgiveness." She gave her mother a quick peck on the cheek. "Pray for me, okay?"

Her father was sitting in his chair, staring out the window when she walked up behind him. Dina reached out and wrapped her arms around him then kissed his forehead. "Hi, Daddy. How are you feeling today?"

He turned with a look of surprise. "I thought you were at the hospital."

"I was earlier. I'm making some major changes in my life, but I don't want to talk about those. Mom will fill you in on them later. I want to talk about us, you and me." She knelt before him and cupped his hands in hers. "I've wronged you, Daddy, and I'm sorry—so sorry for the disrespectful way I've treated you. I've said things to hurt your feelings and I've gone weeks without even speaking to you. I had no right to behave that way. You're my father and I'm so thankful for you. I know I don't deserve it, but can you find it in your heart to forgive me? I love you and I want you to love me."

Her crusty, vindictive father began to weep. "I love you, too, daughter. I'm the one who should be asking for forgiveness. I've been so caught up in my pitiful physical condition, I haven't been the dad to you I should have been. I've been pretty rotten to your mom, too. I'm surprised she hasn't left me by now."

"We've both been at fault, Daddy. Can we start over? Begin anew?"

He pulled her back up to him then wrapped his arms around her, his tears flowing once again. "I'd like that. I've missed my little girl."

"I'm getting married, Daddy, to the man I've been taking care of for the past two weeks."

He brightened. "Married, huh? I kind of wondered if something more than his physical therapy was keeping you in Belmar. You haven't known him long. Is that man worthy of you? You're pretty special."

"Oh, yes. He's a wonderful man. You'll like him. Our wedding will be in Belmar. I want you and Mom to come.

You have to give me away."

"If *you* love him enough to marry him, I'm sure I'll like him, and I'll be proud to give you away."

Dina kissed his cheek once again then rose. "Gotta go, Dad. I've got a full day ahead of me."

"I love you, Dina."

"I love you, Dad."

With a quick good-bye to her mother, Dina rushed out the door, into her car, ready to go back to her apartment to call Will one more time just to hear his voice, and begin packing.

At six the next morning, she headed west on I-70, singing along with the radio and praising God for the two special men in her life. Will, the man she was going to marry, and her father.

❧

Will opened his eyes as the sound of a vehicle came closer and closer. It had to be Dina. As the familiar-looking car came to a stop, he let out a yelp.

❧

Dina was so excited she could barely find the door handle after she turned off the key. Leaping out, she ran to the porch and up the steps, right into Will's arms. "I love, love, love you!" she told him, looping her arms about his neck.

She reached up and, after cupping his face in her hands, gazed into his blue, blue eyes. "I meant every word I said. I love you, my sweet Will, and I want to spend the rest of my life with you."

He bent and kissed her. "I can't believe you're actually here, sweetheart."

"Well, I am and I'm here to stay." She tilted her head and gave him a flirtatious grin. "You do want to marry me, don't you? Or have you changed your mind?"

"Yes, I mean no. I mean yes, I want to marry you and no, I

haven't changed my mind." He pulled her close with his good arm and gazed down at her with eyes of love. "I'm the happiest man alive. You have no idea how much I love you, my darling. No more bull riding. You have my word on it and, trust me, I never go back on my word."

"I do trust you, Will, and with God's help, I'll do everything I can to help you."

"If we keep our minds centered on God and live for Him and each other, how can we fail?" He gazed into her eyes for a moment then his lips sought hers and he kissed her again but, this time, with a kiss unlike any of the others they had shared. Though it was as sweet and as loving as any kiss could be, it was also a kiss of promise, of dedication, a bonding kiss, a sealing kiss that promised true love and devotion for the rest of their lives.

"So how soon can we have the wedding?" he asked as their lips parted. "I'd say the sooner the better. I guess you'll want to have it at your church in Omaha."

"No, my darling. I want it here in Belmar, and I want to invite the entire community."

A frown creased his forehead. "But what about your dad? You'll want him there. Will he come all this way?"

A big smile burst forth on her lips. "Yes, and he's already consented to give me away. Oh, Will, I'm so glad that through all of this God revealed to me how I had wronged my dad as much as he had wronged me. And that I should forgive him, apologize to him, and tell him how sorry I am for the way I treated him. We decided to put the past behind us and start all over again with a clean slate. That's why he agreed to come. In fact, he's excited about it, so both of my parents will be here." She gave him a gentle nudge. "You need to forgive your father, too. Carrying that grudge isn't hurting him—it's hurting you."

Will held up his hand between them. "Whoa, let's not get

carried away here. At least your dad stayed with you and your mom. Mine walked out on us. There's a big difference."

"You'll never have true peace if you don't—"

"I didn't say I *wouldn't* forgive him. I just said—"

"I know what you said, and I understand why you feel the way you do, but promise me you'll at least think about it, okay?"

He nodded. "Yeah, okay. I promise, but right now we need to set our wedding date."

Dina smiled up at him. He had agreed to think about it. That was a start. "If the pastor is available, and if the church is, too, I was thinking of two weeks from today."

Will let out a loud, "Two weeks? Yee haw!" then gave his fist a victorious thrust into the air.

She chuckled. "I guess that means you're happy with the date."

"I couldn't be happier. I still think I'm dreaming."

Weaving her fingers through his, Dina led him to the glider then snuggled up close to him when they sat down. "I think we should have an old-fashioned, down-home wedding, with even a few fiddlers to entertain our guests before the wedding starts. Maybe even have it in the city park where there will be room for anyone who wants to come."

"You serious? That could be a whole lot of people."

"I know, but Belmar is your home and it's going to be my home, too. I want everyone to share in our happiness."

"How are we going to seat that many people?"

"Maybe we could ask everyone to bring their lawn chairs." Her exhilaration grew with each thought. "We could decorate the gazebo with dozens of pots of red geraniums, maybe hang hundreds of long streamers of red and white crepe paper from the trees and let them dance in the wind. And you and your best man could wear blue jeans and boots."

His eyes grew wide. "You weren't kidding when you said

you wanted an old-fashioned, down-home wedding! Blue jeans and boots sound much better to me than a formal tuxedo. I'm sure, if Ben consents to being my best man, he'll like being able to wear jeans."

"Since this is my first—last, and only—wedding I want to wear a white gown, and I'd like you to wear a white shirt."

A slight frown wrinkled his brow.

She treated him to a teasing smile. "A *Western-cut, gripper-fastened* white shirt, with that beautiful silver bolo of yours at the neck. And," she added quickly, "of course you'll want to wear that amazing gold and silver belt buckle you won for being Bull Rider of the Year at the Cheyenne Rodeo."

"Now you're talking my language."

"You're not just saying that to please me? You really do like my ideas?"

"Sure I like them. What's not to like?"

"Maybe my attendants can wear boots and red and white gingham square-dance style dresses. Do you think Ben would go along with wearing a gingham shirt to match the girls' dresses?"

"I'm sure he will. He's a city boy now but there's got to be a little bit of rancher left in him."

She clapped her hands with glee. "This is going to be so much fun, a wedding to remember. I'm so anxious to meet your brothers. Do you think both Jason and Ben will be able to come? Teresa, too? I want her to be my bridesmaid."

"No way would they miss their big brother's wedding. Count on it. They'll be here."

Smiling up at him, Dina rested her head on his shoulder. "I love you, my sweet cowboy."

"I love you, too, babe."

"You haven't changed your mind about giving up bull riding? No regrets?"

He gave her a mischievous smile as his hand rose to pat her cheek. "Not a one. You're cuter than any bull I've ever seen."

She jabbed him in his ribs. "Thanks for the compliment."

Seriousness replaced his smile. "All kidding aside, I can honestly say giving up that part of my life was the right decision. God brought us together, dearest, and I know—as long as we keep our marriage centered around Him and His Word—He will keep us together."

"I know He will, too."

"Someday, my precious one, trust me, I *am* going to build a house for us."

"And our kids?"

He chucked her chin playfully. "At least a dozen, but half of them have to be boys. I'm going to need help on this ranch."

She loved his sense of humor and she loved him. "I have a favor to ask."

"Ask away. For you, I'd do anything."

"If I cleaned them up real good, would you wear your spurs to our wedding?"

He frowned. "Why?"

"Remember that day at the hospital when you told me to leave, go back to Omaha?"

"How could I forget? Telling you to leave was the hardest thing I've ever had to do."

"If I hadn't had your spurs in my car, I would have run out of there and never looked back. But I knew how much they meant to you and I couldn't leave without making sure I got them back to you." She lifted her hand and cupped his cheek. "Those spurs and the kiss we shared that day are what brought us together." She laughed. "Besides, I'm marrying a cowboy. Remember what you told me? A cowboy isn't a cowboy without his spurs."

He tapped her nose with the tip of his finger. "Then I'll wear them!"

fifteen

A little past nine the next morning, while she and Mrs. Martin were in the living room discussing wedding plans, Dina heard Will's new cell phone ring. She hoped it was Pastor Harris responding to the message about their wedding they had left on his voicemail.

"Dina, sweetheart! You'll never believe what happened! Talk about an answer to prayer!" Will came hobbling into the room, his face blanketed with a broad smile. "Dr. Farha just called from Denver with great news! Both he and Dr. Flaming, as well as Dr. Grimes, have decided not to bill me for their part of my surgery! They're all three doing it pro bono. Isn't that amazing? Now the only cost I'll have to worry about will be the hospital bill!"

Her heart thundering with excitement at his news, Dina's jaw dropped as she stared at him. "He actually said that?"

"Sure did. Now, with what my insurance will pay and the help I'll receive from the Rodeo Contestant Crisis Fund, hopefully, the hospital will let me pay out the remainder in monthly installments."

She ran to him and threw her arms about his neck. "Oh, Will, that's such good news. I know how concerned you've been about paying those doctor and hospital bills. See, God is able to perform miracles. We just have to have faith in Him."

Will cupped her cheek with his hand and smiled down at her. "I shouldn't have been surprised. He's already performed one unbelievable miracle in my life. He brought you back to me."

❧

The next two weeks were a whirlwind of activity as Dina worked to get everything ready for their wedding and still have time for Will's therapy. Fortunately, her mother and father arrived a few days early to help, as well as to get acquainted with their soon-to-be son-in-law and his relatives, and attend the rehearsal dinner.

Finally Dina and Will's big day arrived.

❧

Being careful not to muss her lovely white wedding gown, Dina pulled back the flap on the tent that had been set up to serve as the bride's dressing room and peeked out at the area of Belmar's city park where she and Will would soon be pledging their love and their lives to one another. From the looks of the crowd that had gathered, the entire community had turned out for their wedding as she'd hoped.

Her gaze went to her beloved as he stood at the little altar Brian Canter had made for them, straight and tall in his new blue jeans and white Western-cut shirt, the hammered silver bolo about his neck, and the gold and silver rodeo belt buckle at his waist. Just the sight of him made her heartbeat quicken. How handsome he was, and how different he looked from the man she'd met on the road that day. She loved his short hair and Vandyke beard.

She turned when someone touched her on the arm. "You look beautiful." It was Burgandi. "I'm so happy for you. You and Billy Bob—or should I say *Will*—make the perfect couple."

"She's right," Teresa agreed, smiling as she gave Dina a hug. "You're going to be the sister I always wanted. Welcome to the family."

"And you'll be the sister I never had. Will has told me so much about you." Dina lightly kissed her cheek. "I have a feeling we're going to be great friends."

As the music from the portable keyboard sounded, Burgandi grabbed Teresa's hand. "There's our cue. Time for us to go."

"Ready, daughter?"

Dina smiled down at her father as he moved the little lever, nudging his electric wheelchair closer to her. "Oh, yes, Daddy, more than ready." She bent and kissed the top of his balding head then reached out and grasped his free hand, giving it an affectionate squeeze. "I—I love you, Dad." She nearly cried as tears welled up in his eyes.

By the time she and her father reached the gazebo, she thought her face would crack from smiling. Never had she been so happy.

"And who gives this woman to be married to this man?" Pastor Harris asked after Dina and her father had joined Will, Ben and Teresa, Burgandi, the ring bearer, and the flower girl at the altar.

"Her mother and I," Mr. Spark answered proudly, his voice breaking as tears again trailed down his cheeks. "I'm her father."

Dina swallowed at the gaggle of emotions surging through her as she watched him back his wheelchair away and roll up next to her mother who was seated on the front row opposite Will's mother.

She was grateful when Will, seeming to sense the emotions running through her at that moment, reached out and took her hand in his. And once again, she was filled with happiness. She leaned into him, loving his presence, absorbing his strength. He was everything she could ever want in a husband and, best of all, he loved her with an undying, unselfish love, a love of which she could only try to feel worthy.

She listened intently as the soloist sang one of hers and

Will's favorite songs, "You Are the Wind Beneath My Wings," as well as another of their favorites, then to Pastor Harris as he read several scripture passages. All the while she gazed into the face of her beloved.

When it came time to say their vows, Will went first. Though he hadn't had the kind of education most men had, the words he had written were sweeter than any poem she had ever read or heard, and the way he recited them to her made her know they were coming from his heart. She wanted to etch them on her own heart and remember them forever.

Next, she said hers. When she'd been rehearsing them, they'd been merely words she was trying to memorize. But as she gazed into his eyes and slowly repeated them to the one she loved, the words took on new meaning and became the mantra she knew she would strive to live by for the rest of her life.

After one more song and the exchanging of their rings, Pastor Harris again reminded them of what God expected from them as partners with each other and with Him. Then holding his hands over the pair, he said, "William Robert Martin, you may kiss your bride."

Dina suddenly felt breathless. The man who had been kissing her for the past several weeks had been first a patient, then a friend, next her boyfriend, after that, her fiancé. Now, he would be kissing her as—praise the Lord—her husband. She melded into him as he pulled her into his arms, lifting her face toward his. When she felt his lips touch hers, she threw her arms about his neck, twining her fingers through his short hair, and surrendered herself fully to his kiss. When it finally ended, she drew back, even more breathless, still holding on to him for fear her knees would give way and she would end up crumpled at his feet.

"Now, would you please turn and face those who have

come to witness the blending of your two hearts into one," Pastor Harris asked, smiling at the newlyweds after he'd prayed a prayer of dedication.

As Dina started to move, Will tightened his grip on her and nodded toward his feet. She stared down then threw back her head with a boisterous laugh. "You did wear your spurs! I wasn't sure you would."

"Yeah, I might look pretty silly to everyone else but I really liked your idea of wearing them. If it weren't for these old spurs we might not have gotten together."

"You told me a cowboy isn't a cowboy without his spurs. This is one more thing we can tell our grandchildren when we grow old."

Pastor Harris asked their audience to rise. Smiling at the couple, he announced, "By the power vested in me by the State of Nebraska, I now pronounce you husband and wife. Friends and loved ones, it is my privilege to introduce to you—Mr. and Mrs. William Robert Martin. May God bless their union."

Dear Reader,

If you're like me, sometimes we just can't understand why God allows certain things to happen. As I write this dedication, my lovely Christian daughter, Dari Lynn, the mother of twelve beautiful children, all of whom she has home-schooled, is nearly bedfast and will be unable to walk for many months to come. You see, four weeks ago, early on a Sunday morning (when there was absolutely no traffic) while riding her bicycle, she was hit by a hit-and-run driver, dragged by his car several feet, and ended up with both of the large bones in her lower right leg shattered, her knee cap fractured and pushed about six inches above where it should be, as well as other injuries. Already it has required two surgeries and a large metal plate to try to put her leg back together again, not to mention the pain and suffering this accident has caused. Once all of that has healed, she has to have a complete knee replacement. The way things look, the young man who hit her will not even be charged, and there will be no insurance coverage.

Hard to understand, right? But God is faithful. Somehow things will all work out; we know they will. Isn't that what faith is all about? When things like this happen, what would we do if we didn't have the Lord to turn to? If Satan thought this would cause Dari to doubt, he was wrong! Her faith is stronger than ever. With the help of family, her wonderful church family, her friends, her amazing children and husband, and the prayers of all who have heard about her accident, she'll make it! She's a child of the *King*!

How strong is your faith? Does your anchor hold when the storms of life assail? Are you a child of the King? I pray so. I know I couldn't make it without Him.

Your friend,
Joyce Livingston

A Letter To Our Readers

Dear Reader:
In order that we might better contribute to your reading enjoyment, we would appreciate your taking a few minutes to respond to the following questions. We welcome your comments and read each form and letter we receive. When completed, please return to the following:

Fiction Editor
Heartsong Presents
PO Box 719
Uhrichsville, Ohio 44683

1. Did you enjoy reading *The Groom Wore Spurs* by Joyce Livingston?
   ☐ Very much! I would like to see more books by this author!
   ☐ Moderately. I would have enjoyed it more if
   ____
   ____
   ____

2. Are you a member of **Heartsong Presents**? ☐ Yes ☐ No
   If no, where did you purchase this book? ____________
   ____

3. How would you rate, on a scale from 1 (poor) to 5 (superior), the cover design? ____________

4. On a scale from 1 (poor) to 10 (superior), please rate the following elements.

   ____ Heroine
   ____ Hero
   ____ Setting
   ____ Plot
   ____ Inspirational theme
   ____ Secondary characters

5. These characters were special because? ____________________

____

____

6. How has this book inspired your life? ____________________

____

____

7. What settings would you like to see covered in future **Heartsong Presents** books? ____________________

____

____

8. What are some inspirational themes you would like to see treated in future books? ____________________

____

____

9. Would you be interested in reading other **Heartsong Presents** titles? ❑ Yes ❑ No

10. Please check your age range:

❑ Under 18	❑ 18-24
❑ 25-34	❑ 35-45
❑ 46-55	❑ Over 55

Name ____________________

Occupation ____________________

Address ____________________

City, State, Zip ____________________